Eight Away

For more information, visit nzponywriter.com

Email nzponywriter@gmail.com and sign up to my mailing list for exclusive previews, new releases, giveaways and more!

Pony Jumpers
#8

EIGHT AWAY

Kate Lattey

1st Edition (print).

Cover photo: Shutterstock.

This is a work of fiction. Names, characters, places and incidents are either the product of the author's imagination or are used fictitiously.

ISBN-13: 978-1540312433
ISBN-10: 1540312437

- ♥ -

Our greatest glory is not in never falling,
but in rising every time we fall.

Confucius

- ♥ -

1

FALLING

The sun was lowering, casting long shadows behind each of the jumps in the arena. Misty tossed his head impatiently and laid his ears back at the chestnut pony on his left as we waited for instructions.

Bruce fished a pack of cigarettes out of his pocket as he pointed out the course. "Start over the blue oxer, left to the red oxer, four forward strides to the planks, then up the outside line in six."

I saw Susannah nodding, running her eyes over the course as she picked up her reins. On my right, Katy was leaning forward on Molly's neck to retrieve part of her forelock that had slipped under her browband. I twisted my fingers around Misty's rubber reins as Bruce looked at the three of us with narrowed eyes.

Not me first. Please don't pick me first.

"Tess, you're up. You two can fight over who follows her," he told the others. He drew a cigarette out of the pack and slid it between his lips, then nodded at me. "When you're ready."

I wasn't sure that I would ever be ready. The jumps in Susannah's arena were set high on the stands, and no amount of reminding myself that I'd jumped that high many times before was making me feel any calmer. This lesson had started badly, with Misty bucking through the entire warm-up, and had only got worse as we'd progressed onto jumping. Bruce didn't believe in starting slow or small, and had thrown the fences up to full height immediately. Susannah and Katy were loving the challenge, but I was more than ready for this lesson to be over.

I wished I hadn't let my mother talk me into coming. But Susannah had invited me and Katy to join in with her, and Bruce was a former Olympian, so Mum had leapt at the chance, despite her strong dislike for Susannah and her family. I'd never had much success at saying no to my mother, and it was especially difficult right now. She'd dropped me off early this morning before taking my sister Hayley to see a specialist in Palmerston North, making sure that I knew that she was going out of her way to help me, and I'd better be appreciative. I wished she'd just let me stay home.

I pretended to be memorising the course as the other two moved their ponies towards the gate, bickering cheerfully over who would go next. AJ walked between them, one arm still in a sling, the other draped over Skip's neck. She was disappointed to not be able to ride today, but I would've swapped places with her in a heartbeat. Not the broken collarbone, obviously, but just being a spectator looked very appealing to me right now.

Bruce lit his cigarette, watching me shorten my reins and take a deep breath. He'd been putting the pressure on me for the past half hour, seemingly determined to expose me as a complete fraud. As if I needed him to. I was well aware that I wasn't a confident, competent Pony Grand Prix rider like my friends. I was a girl doing what she had to to keep the peace at home, riding my sister's pony because she was sick and might be dying and selling her best friend wasn't an option right now. That meant me riding him, whether I wanted to or not. Plus she still had this crazy idea that I was going to jump Misty in Pony of the Year next month, and what Hayley wanted, Hayley got. So here I was.

I steered Misty in a stampeding trot around the outside of the course, trying not to look at the height of the jumps.

You've jumped bigger, I told myself.

Are you sure?

Just focus. Breathe. Get it over and done with.

I took a breath, then let it out as I did my best to slow Misty's rampage, bringing him onto a smaller circle, slowing my rising, closing my fingers around the reins. The hard crest of his neck rose up in front of me, and I battled with the instinct to shorten my reins. That would only make his head come higher and his neck brace harder against me, and then Bruce would yell at me again. I've never liked being yelled at, have never been one of those people who thrives under a merciless coach who is sparing with compliments. I need someone to reassure me, to tell me that I can do it, to remind me to breathe. But he wasn't here. He was back at the farm, and I wondered what he was doing.

Focus.

What would he tell me to do? I conjured up Jonty's face in front of me, his thick dark hair falling into his eyes, his light brown eyes, his crooked smile.

You've got this.

Easy for him to say. My mind skipped back to yesterday, when he'd been schooling Misty in the home paddock for me. I'd sat there and watched the wilful grey pony trot smoothly across the grass with his neck proudly arched, his paces rhythmic and steady, his curved ears flickering back and forth attentively. I wanted to go back to that moment, to be resting on a sun-warmed oil drum in the middle of our paddock watching my boyfriend ride my pony far better than I ever could. It was a peculiar twist of fate that he had all the talent and none of the opportunity, while I had all the opportunity and no desire to do any of it.

"Sometime today would be good," Bruce called as I trotted past him, and I knew that I couldn't put it off any longer.

Sliding my leg back a fraction, I touched Misty into his boisterous canter, looked at the first fence on the course, sat taller, lowered my hands, and tried to convince my fingers to soften against the thick rubber reins. Misty sped up, and I stared at the painted rails as they approached. My brain froze, and my vision blurred slightly.

Find your distance.

It was all Bruce talked about, and everyone else seemed to be able to do it, but not me. Not when the jumps were this big. I might have gone from falling off Misty every time I jumped him to winning and placing in some big Pony Grand Prix classes in the past few months, but that didn't mean I enjoyed it. I'd convinced myself, somehow, not to think about the height or width of the obstacles, had managed to make my determination to succeed trump my fear of falling, but that didn't mean I wasn't still afraid.

Misty plunged forward, and I checked him instinctively, but I was too late to steady his pace. He threw his head up, took a stutter step in front of the fence and jumped awkwardly. The back rail of the oxer crashed to the ground as we landed, and Misty tucked his head down and bucked hard, telling me off. I dug my knees into the rolls of the saddle and gritted my teeth.

Breathe. Get his head up. Keep going.

"Stop!"

I managed to drag Misty back to a trot as Bruce picked up the pole and replaced it in the cups.

"Start again, and don't just sit there like a zombie. *Ride* your pony. Help him out! You can't wait until the absolute last second to check him." He spoke around the cigarette in the corner of his mouth, then took a long drag from it. "Again. Get it right this time."

I shortened my reins, and Bruce snapped at me. "Quit climbing up his neck. Give him some room to move."

I let the reins out and Misty bounded forward as we approached the oxer again. It looked even bigger than before. Had Bruce put it up higher when he'd replaced the pole? I felt my heart squeeze inside my chest, my breath coming in short gasps. I didn't want to do this.

Every fibre of my being screamed at me to stop, to turn away, to say no. But I kept riding down to the jump with my eyes up and legs on, pretending that I wanted to jump it.

Fake it 'til you make it, right?

This time I let Misty hold his own pace, and we made it over cleanly. I exhaled as we landed and looked around to the next fence.

One down, four to go.

I turned towards the red oxer and Misty plunged forward, dragging the reins through my fingers. I gritted my teeth and forced myself to sit still, waiting for that magic moment when I would see the distance to the jump and be able to check him back or ride him forward or just stay doing what I was doing and get over the fence.

But the distance never showed up. We arrived at the jump completely wrong, and I felt Misty suck back behind the bit, preparing to stop. I couldn't let that happen. I didn't need to give Bruce any more ammunition to yell at me. So I dug my heels in and cracked the short crop I was carrying down onto Misty's shoulder.

"Hup!" I cried, throwing my weight forward and making a grab at Misty's short mane.

Startled by my sudden commitment, the grey pony made an effort to jump, but he was too close to the fence to get over cleanly. He caught his legs on the front rail, and after a heart-stopping moment as he scrambled in mid-air, he fell forward on a head-first trajectory towards the ground. I saw it coming and closed my eyes as I flew over his head, landing hard on my shoulder. The breath was knocked out of me, and I curled instinctively into a ball as the rails fell down around me. I felt the ground in front of me shudder and opened my eyes to see Misty's hoof only centimetres from my face. I watched in terror as he scrambled his way out of the fallen jump, somehow avoiding me with his other three hooves, before closing my eyes again and wishing myself away.

For a brief moment, it worked. I was no longer on my back in the dirt, winded and bruised and defeated. Instead I was at home, standing on my own two feet in the middle of a windswept paddock with long golden grass brushing against my legs, staring out across the hills and valleys that made up our farm. Blobs of white sheep were scattered across the paddocks below, the warm smell of the pine trees wafted down from the hills behind me, and the sun baked my skin as I surveyed the land around me. Home. The only place I wanted to be.

"Are you okay?"

And I was back, looking into AJ's concerned blue eyes. I pushed myself up into a sitting position, adrenalin pumping through my shaking body, and lied to her.

"I'm fine."

AJ reached down a hand to me and I grabbed it, then cried out as she tried to pull me to my feet. My shoulder was badly bruised, and I gasped with pain as I sank back down, tears prickling my eyes. This wasn't how this lesson was supposed to go. I was supposed to be brave and capable and come home ready to compete in Pony of the Year in only three weeks' time. But as usual, nothing was going to plan.

"What do you mean, you fell off?"

Mum glared at me as I led Misty up the ramp of our horse truck, my shoulder still throbbing relentlessly.

"I fell off," I repeated.

Why was she acting as though she was surprised? It was hardly out of the ordinary for me to hit the dirt. Especially off this pony. I thought about how close he'd come to standing on my face, and felt physically sick.

"But you got back on."

I swallowed the bile that was rising in my throat and turned Misty around in the truck, nudging his hindquarters back into the gap between the dividers.

"Tess?"

My hands were shaking as I tied Misty's lead rope to a frayed piece of baling twine attached to the bar. It wouldn't take much for Misty to break that twine – just a quick snap back of his head and he'd be free. But he stood quietly in the truck, his shenanigans forgotten. He knew just as well as I did what the truck meant. Home, dinner, and then bed. But first, I had to go through a full interrogation.

"Tell me you got back on and kept going."

I stepped back and swung the divider over, using my left hand to pull the pin back and my right hip to shove it into place.

"I hurt my shoulder."

"Oh for God's *sake*, Tess. Honestly, sometimes I wonder why I bother. Are you determined to ruin that pony's reputation?"

I saw AJ look up from where she was sitting on the edge of a water trough, saw Katy frown in my direction as she wrapped Molly's legs, saw Susannah's head swivel towards me as they listened to my mother's remonstrations. It was nothing they hadn't heard before. It was nothing I didn't hear on a daily basis

And now I got to sit in the truck and listen to it all the way home.

"Hey you."

I looked up from mixing Misty's feed and felt my heart lift as Jonty walked into the feed room with a smile just for me.

"Hey yourself."

"How was your lesson?"

I picked up the feed bucket with my left hand and pulled a face at him. "Terrible. I fell off."

I saw the sympathy in his eyes, and the lack of judgement that I loved so much about him. He didn't expect me to be the best. He thought I was brave just for trying.

"You hurt yourself?"

"Just my shoulder. Not that it was a good enough excuse for my mum. We had the whole trip home for her to remind me how much of a disappointment I am."

I didn't have to tell him which shoulder I hurt, or have to ask him to carry the heavy bucket for me. He did these things instinctively, his quick eyes noticing every detail around him. Jonty's warm hand slid into mine and our fingers slotted together easily, the way they always did. As though they were made to. My thumb brushed the long scar on the back of his hand.

"Three more weeks," Jonty reminded me as Misty bashed his broad chest against the yard railing, demanding that his dinner be served without further delay.

"Three more weeks," I repeated. Jonty slung the bucket into the yard and Misty shoved his face into it and started eating as though he hadn't seen food in weeks. "If I survive them, that is."

Bad choice of words. We didn't make jokes about survival around here. Not lately. Not since Hayley had been diagnosed with a brain tumour. She'd only just finished her last round of radiation therapy, and here I was making survival jokes.

But Jonty understood. He came over and put his arms around my waist, pulling me in close against him, and I rested my head on his shoulder and watched Misty stuff his face with feed. It was a waiting game to find out whether the radiation had done enough, or whether Hayley was going to need surgery. We were all living on tenterhooks, and I knew that my mother's harsh words to me were due, in large part, to the extreme stress she was under. But it didn't make them any easier to hear.

"She'll be okay."

"I know."

We told each other these lies daily, and pretended to believe them. I closed my eyes and tried to relax, listening only to the sounds of Misty's munching. A slow, creeping sense of peace stole over me, and

I leaned into it, grasping at the promise of serenity.

It didn't last. What had started out as a distant rumble of a quad bike was coming ever closer, and moving quickly. I straightened up and stepped back from Jonty, who reluctantly released me. I shot him an apologetic smile. My parents weren't particularly happy with my choice of boyfriend, and I didn't need my father to turn up and find us mid-embrace. The day had been bad enough already without dealing with his silent, disapproving glares.

But it wasn't Dad on the quad bike that came battering around the corner with two weary farm dogs loping behind it. It was Bayard.

"Oh, great. This day just keeps getting better," I muttered, turning my back on my former best friend and leaning against the yard railing to watch Misty eat. He was pawing at the bucket in feverish delight.

"Don't expect a refill if you tip it all out into the dirt," I warned him as Jonty's arm brushed against mine.

"Should I go home?"

"No. You shouldn't have to," I told him. "It's not your fault that Bayard inexplicably hates you. Let him be the one to go home."

"Looks like he's still got work to do though," Jonty pointed out, looking over his shoulder at Bayard. "And I've got homework."

"A likely excuse. Since when do you do your homework?"

Jonty turned back towards me with a crooked grin. "Maybe I'm turning over a new leaf this year."

"Maybe you're full of crap," I suggested playfully, and his smile widened.

"You love me."

"Lucky for you," I told him.

Jonty stepped in closer and put an arm around me, then kissed my forehead. "Lucky is right."

I could hear Bayard's footsteps approaching from behind us, and the dogs appeared by our side, nudging us eagerly for attention. Jonty let go of me and leaned down to greet them by name.

"Hi Rusk, hi Loki."

"That's Thor." Bayard stopped next to us, a bucket of fencing tools in his hand.

"Oh."

"They look practically identical," I said in Jonty's defence. "I thought it was Loki too, at first."

"Well, they *are* brothers," Jonty said with a wink in my direction, and I grinned.

But Bayard didn't get the joke. "No they're not. They're not even related."

I rolled my eyes. "It was a joke, Bay."

He frowned. "Not a very funny one."

"It is if you know anything about Norse mythology." He just stared at me blankly, and I shook my head. "Never mind."

I turned my back on them both and looked at Misty, who was kicking his bucket around the yard in disappointment that he'd finished his feed. "Right, are you done?"

"Looks like it," Jonty confirmed. "I'll put him out for you, if you want. Save you trying to chuck a cover on with your sore shoulder."

I smiled at him. "You're my hero."

Bayard snorted disparagingly and marched into the barn without another word. The two Huntaways followed him loyally to the door, then lay down to wait for his return. Jonty led my angry pony across the yard towards the paddock, and I leaned on the fence and carefully kneaded my shoulder, trying to figure out whether it was strained or just badly bruised. Either way, I was going to have to get back on him tomorrow. I dreaded the thought.

"Tess!"

I looked across to the house, where the porch light had just come on. My mother was silhouetted in the doorway, staring in my direction. I felt the same surge in my chest that always accompanied someone yelling my name these days. Far too many times it had been the precursor to calamity, to Hayley having a seizure, to another ambulance call out, another overnight stay in hospital, another day or two before she could come home and we could all continue with the pretence that we were living some kind of normal life, all of us waiting with bated breath for it to happen again.

I found my voice. "What?"

"Hurry up, would you? Your dinner's getting cold."

I felt my entire body sag in relief. I wasn't sure how much longer we could all live like this, always on the edge, waiting for disaster to strike.

Knowing that it was only a matter of time.

2

FIRST PERIOD

I nudged my locker shut with my shoulder as the bell rang, and struggled to shove my Biology textbook into my backpack. There was a tight cluster of younger girls in crisp new uniforms standing in my way, and I shrugged my bag onto my good shoulder as I looked for a way past them.

"Someone should tell her."

"Bags not!"

"Ew, no way!"

They were staring at someone behind me, and I looked over my shoulder to see another young girl with her back to us. It took me a moment to notice the dark stain on the back of the girl's skirt, and I winced in sympathy. Not what you wanted when you'd just started high school. I felt for her, but I was going to be late for my class if I didn't get a move on.

Then she turned around, and I recognised her tear-streaked face at once.

"Bella!"

Jonty's sister looked simultaneously embarrassed and relieved to see me. She wiped at the tears on her cheeks as I hurried to her side, all hesitation gone. I put my good arm around her shoulders and gave them a gentle squeeze.

"Come with me."

Bella sniffled, but didn't resist as I started steering her towards the other end of the corridor. "Where are we going?"

"To the nurse. She'll give you another skirt to borrow for today."

Bella took a shaky breath, walking alongside me with her head still bowed, then spoke so softly that I almost missed her words.

"Do you have any...stuff?"

I knew what she meant, and shook my head regretfully. "Not with me, sorry," I replied. "Don't you?"

She shook her head, and it finally dawned on me. "Is this your first time?" Bella's chin wobbled, and my heart went out to her. "Aw, don't worry. The nurse will sort you out. I'm sure she's fully prepared for this kind of thing."

We reached the end of the corridor and I pushed the door open into the main courtyard. Bella baulked at the sight of so many students still milling around.

"Here." I reached into my backpack and pulled out my jersey. "Tie this around your waist, then nobody will be able to tell."

Bella took it with a doubtful expression. "Are you sure? What if it gets..." She couldn't bring herself to finish the sentence, but I just shook my head at her.

"I'm not worried, I can wash it. Go on."

Bella tied the jersey around her waist to hide the stain on her skirt and walked with me towards the office, her head held higher now. But her steps faltered again when she saw Jonty walking in our direction with a couple of his mates. He noticed us, and broke away from his friends. His surprised smile dimmed as he saw the tear-stains on Bella's cheeks.

"Everything okay?"

"Yeah. We're just going to the office. No worries."

Jonty looked at me, then back to his sister. "What happened?"

Bella kept her eyes on the ground, refusing to look at her brother.

"It's fine," I told him. "Trust me. I'll take care of her."

Jonty still looked concerned, his eyes flickering quickly between the pair of us. He was very protective of his sisters, and I knew it took an effort for him to walk away and leave her in my hands when she was clearly upset.

"You sure?" he asked her, and Bella nodded emphatically.

"I'm all right," she mumbled. "Tess is helping me."

Jonty shot me a doubtful look, and I smiled reassuringly at him. "It's all good. Just go to class. We'll talk later."

Jonty nodded, leaned in and kissed the corner of my mouth before hurrying after his mates, who were hooting appreciatively. I ignored them, putting a hand on Bella's back as we walked on.

She glanced at the boys behind her. "Are they laughing at me?"

"Nope, they're laughing at your brother."

"You won't really tell him, will you?" She looked up at me, her big brown eyes so much like his.

"Not if you really don't want me to," I said. "But he's pretty nosy, so if I don't, he'll just start pestering you about it. Let me know if that's a conversation you want to have."

She cringed as we reached the administration building, and I pulled the door open. "Can't he just mind his own business?"

"Not his strong suit," I said, following her into the building. "He's *your* brother, so surely you know that by now."

"I guess."

The front desk was abandoned, and the door to the nurse's office was shut. I hesitated for a moment, wondering what to do next, until a harassed-looking teacher came out of a nearby room with an armload of papers and spotted us.

"What are you girls doing in here? You should be in class."

"We need to see the nurse," I told her.

"Both of you?"

I glanced at Bella's worried face and knew I couldn't abandon her now. "Yes."

The teacher pursed her lips as she rapped on the nurse's door it, then opened it a few inches and peered in. "Two girls here to see you." She nodded, and shut the door again. "She's with a student right now. Wait there," she told us, pointing at a row of chairs against the wall before striding away.

I took a seat, and Bella followed suit, her eyes still on the floor.

"Don't feel too bad about it," I told her. "Happens to us all."

She looked at me dubiously. "Has this happened to you?"

"Not exactly," I admitted. "My first time was even worse." Bella looked sceptical, so I explained. "I was at a horse show."

"Oh." She thought for a moment, then her eyes widened. "Were you wearing white jodhpurs?"

"Cream ones, which is just as bad," I told her, feeling my cheeks flush slightly at the recollection of that day. "And I didn't even realise until I'd jumped my round. Came out of the ring feeling quite pleased with myself because we'd gone clear, then Hayley met me at the gate and told me. I was so embarrassed."

"Did she laugh at you?" Bella asked, her eyes darkening.

"No, she was actually nice about it," I said. "Took me back to the truck and found me some stuff, gave me some of her jodhs to borrow. I didn't want to go back for the jump off, but she made me do it."

Bella's face had turned hopeful, looking for a happy ending. "Did you win?"

"No. I fell off."

"Oh." Bella scuffed the lino with the toe of her battered shoe. "That's a shame."

"Happens to me a lot," I admitted to her as my shoulder throbbed, like it had suddenly remembered that it was sore.

Bella scoffed. "But you're such a good rider."

"Not really."

"Yes you are. Jonty says you are, and he knows."

"He's just being nice," I told her, but she shook her head.

"No he's not. He said…"

But before I could find out what it was that Jonty had told her, the nurse's door opened and a tall boy with a bandaged hand walked out, followed by a large woman with dark red hair in a nurse's smock.

"What can I do for you girls?"

I explained the situation as quickly as I could, relieved to see the sympathetic look on her face.

"Oh dear. Don't worry love, we'll get you sorted out," she told Bella kindly. "Come with me now." She looked over at me. "Thanks for bringing her in. You can go to class now."

That didn't sound like a request, so I stood up. "Okay." I looked at Bella. "You'll be all right now?"

She nodded, biting her lip. "Yeah. Thank you."

"No worries. That's what friends are for."

Bella's eyes lit up at my words, and she broke into a wide smile, then flung her arms around me in a tight hug. Surprised, I hugged her back.

"I'll see you on the bus later, okay?"

"Okay." Bella turned and followed the nurse into her office, and I finally went to class.

"I believe this is yours."

I was standing on one leg and pulling my jodhpur boot on with one hand when my school jersey flew through the air and hit me in the face.

"Nice throw," I told Jonty as he came into the tack room.

"Hey, you caught it, didn't you?" He sat on the tack box in front of me and drummed his fingers against the worn wood. "So now that I've got you alone at last," he continued with a lifted eyebrow, "are you going to tell me what was going on with Bella today? Because she's refusing to spill."

I put my foot on the tack box next to his hip and zipped up my leather chap. "Maybe you don't need to know," I teased him. "Maybe it's our little secret."

"Yours and Bella's?"

"Sure, why not?" I returned my foot to the floor and couldn't help smiling at his disappointed expression. "Look, it's not a big deal, honestly. Bella was just…experiencing some women's problems," I said delicately, folding my jersey and putting it on the table behind me.

Jonty frowned. "She what? What's that supposed to… Oh." I turned around in time to catch the look on his face as he caught on. "And she needed your help?"

"Let's just say she had a leakage issue, and leave it at that," I told him, unable to suppress a grin at his horrified expression. "Hey, you wanted to know."

"Yeah, yeah, okay." He threw his hands up and got to his feet. "I've heard enough."

I laughed. "Told you not to be so nosy."

"Lesson learned." He reached past me to take Copper's bridle off the wall. Hayley wasn't allowed to start riding again yet, and Jonty had been working her big chestnut horse for her while she was out of action. "You ready to ride today?"

No. Not remotely. "Yeah. But can we just go for a quiet hack? My shoulder's still pretty sore."

It was true, but it wasn't the real problem. The nerves that I'd somehow managed to overcome in the past few months were back with a vengeance, and the thought of getting on Misty was making me feel physically sick.

"Of course we can." His brow furrowed as he noticed my expression. "You okay?"

"Yeah."

I couldn't fool him though. He always saw straight through me.

"Nervous?"

"How'd you guess?"

He slung Copper's bridle over his shoulder and put his hands on my waist. "I'm a mind-reader."

"Oh yeah? What am I thinking right now?"

"I don't want to say." He pulled me in closer, bowing his head until our foreheads were touching. "I wouldn't want to make you blush."

"Too late."

He laughed softly as he leaned in and kissed me. His arms tightened around my waist and I closed my eyes, reaching up to cradle the back of his neck with one hand as I deepened the kiss.

"Would you two get a room?"

Jonty and I jerked apart and turned to look at Hayley, standing in the doorway.

"We're *in* a room," Jonty told her with a grin.

"A room without me in it," Hayley clarified. She was leaning one shoulder against the door frame, and I tried not to notice the dark circles under her eyes, and how exhausted she looked. "Do you think you can take your tongue out of my sister's mouth for long enough to tell me how Copper's going?" she asked Jonty.

"Behaving himself, most of the time."

"Have you jumped him lately?" Hayley glanced at me, a sudden spark coming back in her eyes. "That was a question for Jonty. No need to ask *you* that question after what I just witnessed."

"Shut up," I told her as Jonty gave a traitorous laugh.

"Not lately," he admitted to my sister, but his eyes lit up in anticipation of what was coming next. Part of the deal was that he was only allowed to jump Copper under Hayley's supervision. Since Jonty rode the horse ten times better than Hayley did anyway, it seemed overly controlling to me, but that had always been Hayley's style. She liked to have everyone under her thumb.

Stop it, I told myself as I picked up Misty's saddle with my good arm. *She's sick. Be grateful she's still here to annoy and embarrass you.*

"You can jump him today, if you want," Hayley said casually, and I knew that a quiet hack was definitely off the cards now. There was no way I was taking Misty into the hills alone, but there was equally no way Jonty would turn down the chance to put Copper over a few fences. And if I joined them in the paddock, Hayley would expect me to jump too.

"What do you say, Tess?"

How could I say no?

"Fine by me."

I had to jump again eventually, and the sooner I got back on the horse – literally – the better.

Right?

I watched nervously as Jonty sat the pole on top of the two barrels, making a jump barely over a metre high. I'd been over it a hundred times before, but today it suddenly seemed immense. *You don't have to jump it,* I reminded myself. *They can't make you.*

I lifted the saddle flap and tightened the girth a notch, dodging Misty's teeth as he attempted an indignant nip.

"Be nice," I told the pony as I gathered my reins up into my left hand and prepared to mount. "Just for once, please. Be nice to me."

I could hear Jonty talking to my sister as he came to take Copper from her, laughing at something she said. He swung lightly into the saddle and leaned down to check his girth, while I grasped Misty's stirrup with my right hand and angled it towards me, doing my best to ignore the ache in my shoulder and the churning in my stomach. I felt physically sick, and my hands were shaking.

Just get on with it.

I tried. But as I lifted my left foot an inch from the ground, my right knee went weak and buckled. The strength disappeared from my body and I grabbed a fistful of Misty's mane, sagging against the saddle.

"Come on Tess, get on your pony and stop mucking about," Hayley said impatiently.

I tried again, but this time I couldn't even lift my left foot. It was unnerving, as though I was suddenly paralysed, and sheer panic set in. I forced myself to move, just to prove to myself that I still had control of my own body. I let go of Misty's mane and stepped back to the end of his reins, my legs trembling. The grey pony turned his head and gave me an irritated look, wondering why I insisted on wasting so much of his time.

Copper's shadow fell over me, and I looked up at Jonty, staring down at me with concern in his brown eyes.

"You okay?"

I shook my head. "No. Not really."

"What's wrong?"

"I don't know." I swallowed hard as he slid down from Copper's back and put an arm around me.

"Just ignore her," Hayley snapped impatiently from behind us, where she was perched on an overturned barrel. "She's just being a drama queen as usual."

We both ignored her. "I can't make myself get on," I told Jonty, my voice trembling around the words.

Jonty's breath was warm against my cheek. "D'you want a leg up?"

I took a breath, and nodded. *Fake it 'til you make it.* "Okay."

"On three."

I stepped back in towards Misty and shortened the reins, then placed my hands on the top of the saddle. My right shoulder screamed in agony, and I pulled it back down with a yelp, cradling it against my side.

"Oh for crying out loud," Hayley grumbled.

"Ignore her," Jonty said softly in my ear. "You can do this. Just use one arm." He reached down and grabbed my calf, bending my knee and preparing to boost me into the saddle. My right leg wobbled precariously as I balanced on it. "One, two…"

But it was too late. The memories I'd been trying to suppress broke through my mental barriers and flooded into my head like a tidal wave, each memory crashing harder against me than the last. The suspended moment of impending doom…the crash of falling poles…the searing pain in my shoulder…the hoof in front of my face that seemed closer every time I remembered it, missing me by the barest inch…

"No!"

I pulled away from him, away from Misty, and staggered a couple of steps before bending over and vomiting into the grass. My whole body was shaking like a leaf, and my skin was clammy and cold. I could hear Hayley asking questions as I felt Jonty's hand on the small of my back, reassuring me that it was okay.

But it wasn't okay. Because I'd been nervous before, but this was something completely different. I wasn't just scared to ride.

I was terrified.

3

FAMILY

The cicadas were ringing in my ears as Jonty and I walked down the road, my hand clasped tightly in his. He'd been talking, trying to reassure me at first, then just chattering about inconsequential things. I'd pretended to listen, but I don't think either of us were fooled. My thoughts swirled anxiously around in my head, battling furiously for my attention. I'd failed. I hadn't been able to get back on Misty, and no amount of gentle coaxing from Jonty – or much less gentle antagonising from Hayley – had changed my mind. In the end I'd taken the grey pony back to the barn and unsaddled him while Jonty jumped Copper. That hadn't gone particularly well either, and Hayley had lost interest after a few minutes anyway. The whole afternoon had been a disaster.

My footsteps slowed as we approached the cottage where Jonty's family lived. His scruffy black pony Taniwha was grazing the strip on the opposite side of the road, swishing his long tail at the flies biting his flanks, and I could hear one of his sisters squealing from inside the house. His hand loosened its grip on mine, and instinctively, I closed my fingers tighter, holding him by my side.

"You're gonna be okay." Jonty stopped walking, pulled me in towards him and held me tight. "You got spooked, that's all. It's not the end of the world."

I rested my head on his shoulder, wanting so badly to believe him.

"I don't like being scared."

"I know." He kissed the side of my head. "But you've talked yourself out of it before. Maybe you can do it again."

I shook my head. "I was just pretending."

"Still worked, didn't it?" he asked.

"Yeah, but I don't know if I can do it again. I don't know if I can make myself believe."

He held me closer, his cheek against my hair. "You'll never know unless you try. We'll work through this, okay? Start slow, get back on Rory now that she's all healed up from her injury. Or one of the station hacks, they're all dead quiet. You don't have to get straight back on Misty. Take it a day at a time, see how you go."

"Mum's going to be so mad at me."

I felt his chest rise and fall as he sighed. "That's her problem," he replied. "Not yours. Maybe it's her fault for trying to make you do something you didn't want to."

I sniffled. "I'll tell her that," I said. We both knew that I wouldn't, but we could pretend.

"You go right ahead."

I took a deep breath, then slowly let it out before reluctantly extracting myself from Jonty's embrace.

"I guess I should go home and face the music."

His dark hair tumbled forward. It was almost long enough to touch his eyelashes, and I wondered how long it would be before someone at school made him cut it to regulation length.

"Come say hi to Murray first," Jonty said coaxingly. "He's been dying to meet you."

"Is that right?"

"Won't shut up about it," he insisted. "All I hear, all day long, is *Why are you holding out on me? When are you going to introduce me to Tess?*"

His hand gripped mine again as he led me towards the small,

ramshackle cottage that sat on the edge of the dirt road. The broken window in the front room had been boarded up, and the broken guttering on the roof had been propped back into place, but the whole structure still looked like it was only standing on a wing and a prayer. I felt uneasy coming here. The cottage was owned by my parents, and they were the ones allowing Jonty's family to live in such poor conditions. But whenever I tried to bring it up with them, Mum would remind me that they barely paid rent, and if they wanted a better standard of living they should move back into town and rent a real house. Dad didn't usually say anything, but he didn't disagree with her either. She was still mad at him for letting the Fishers move in in the first place, but they'd turned up on our doorstep at Christmas four years ago with literally nowhere else to go. It was supposed to be temporary, a week or two at most, just so they had a roof over their heads. It still wasn't much of a roof, but they'd been under it ever since.

Hand-in-hand, we walked around the side of the building to where a black and white goat was balancing on top of a cardboard apple box, nibbling on a pair of jeans that hung from the nearby clothesline.

"Murray!" Jonty let go of my hand and ran towards the goat, which immediately let go of the jeans and jumped off the box, hightailing it across the back lawn. "You little punk!"

Unfortunately for Murray, he'd failed to realise that he was still chained up, and was quickly brought to a sharp halt when he hit the end of his chain. Immediately changing his game plan, the little goat lowered his head and charged at Jonty, who sidestepped, then grabbed the goat's short horns in his hands and turned him around.

"You…" he told the animal, "were supposed to make a good impression." He looked over his shoulder at me with his crooked smile, the wiry muscles in his arms standing out as he wrestled with the animal. "He's still learning some manners. I've been trying to teach him, but…" Jonty shrugged helplessly as I walked towards them.

"Can't teach what you don't know," I pointed out.

"Ouch, Tess. That stings." Jonty put a hand over his heart and pretended to look emotionally wounded. Murray seized his opportunity and renewed his efforts to butt against Jonty's leg, but was held firmly in check. "Quit it, you. Don't you know when to accept defeat?"

"Apparently he's a slow learner."

I resisted the urge to follow that up with a crack about animals being like their owners as Murray finally quit struggling and turned to look at me.

"Murray, this is Tess," Jonty told him. "Be nice to her, okay?" Murray bleated feebly, and Jonty looked him firmly in the eye. "Promise?" The goat bleated again, and Jonty nodded. "Okay."

He let Murray go, watching suspiciously as the goat walked up to me and started nibbling gently at the hem of my shorts. I scratched his head between his horns, and he leaned into my touch.

"I think he likes you."

"I think he definitely likes me better than you," I grinned as the back door of the cottage slammed shut, and Jonty's youngest sister Phoebe came towards us, barefoot across the unkempt grass.

Jonty was quick to question her. "Phoebes, did you leave this box out here?"

She stopped, looking at the apple carton, then nodded. "I brought it home from the supermarket yesterday for Murray. He likes to stand on it. Hi Tess."

"Hi."

"Yeah, stand on it and eat my clothes," Jonty told her, going to the clothesline and unpegging his jeans. "Look what he's done!" He held up the left leg, which had been well-chewed around the ankle, and glared at Phoebe.

I caught her guilty expression, and felt bad for her.

"I don't know about you, Phoebe, but I can't see a difference," I said. "Can you?"

She grinned and shook her head, and Jonty pulled a face at me. "Your manners are worse than my goat's."

"*My* goat!" Phoebe insisted, running forward and putting her arms around Murray's scrawny neck, which he tolerated surprisingly well.

"If he's your goat, teach him to behave himself," Jonty told her.

Phoebe just rolled her eyes at him. "He's a *goat,* Jonty."

He grinned. "Right. What was I thinking?"

"That you Jonty?"

We both looked over at the house, where Jonty's mother was standing in the back doorway, one hand on her hip and staring at us. Well, mostly at me. She was a solidly-built woman with thick dark hair that was always tied back, and spidery tattoos on both of her bare arms.

"Who else would it be?" he asked. "Mum, you remember Tess."

"Of course. How are you?" she said politely, looking uncomfortable at being confronted unexpectedly by her landlord's daughter.

"I'm fine thanks. How're you?"

"Oh we're just fine." She glanced around the yard, and stepped a little further out of the house, blocking my view of the interior. "We just love it here. I, uh…we're very grateful to have this place."

I could sense Jonty's unease building next to me, and tried to reassure them all with my words. "It's no problem, really. It's not like we were using it."

After I'd spoken, I knew that hadn't been the right thing to say. A moment of awkward silence lingered around us, then Jonty's mum turned to her son.

"Jonty, would you dig up some spuds for us tonight?"

"Yeah, sure." He grabbed a garden fork that was hanging from a couple of nails on the back wall of the cottage, then looked at me.

"Come help?"

"Uh, sure."

I could feel his mother's and sister's eyes on me as I followed him to the other side of the house, where the vege garden was. Jonty stopped at the edge of the row of potato plants and shoved the fork into the ground, loosening the soil around the plants.

"I should probably go."

He looked up at me, crouched in the dirt on the edge of the garden. "Why?"

"I don't know. It's awkward, isn't it?"

He frowned. "Nah, it's all good. You're welcome to stay for a bit. Join us for dinner if you want." He pulled out a large potato, and grinned at me. "I hope you like spuds."

"Thanks, but I'm not sure your mum'll be okay with that."

"Why not?" He held the potato out towards me, and I instinctively took it. He started digging around again, searching for more. "She likes you."

I glanced back at the cottage suspiciously. "I'm pretty sure *that's* not true."

Jonty frowned. "Course it is. She's just a bit nervous, that's all. She wants you to like her."

"Of course I like her."

"So stay and eat with us." I opened my mouth to argue as he passed me two more potatoes, then met my eyes with a pleading expression. "Please?"

I sighed. "How do you do that?"

He squinted at me, confused. "Do what?"

"You give me that *look*." His eyebrows lifted as I shook my head at him. "You turn those puppy dog eyes on me and I can't say no."

Jonty grinned even wider, rocking back onto his heels. "You wanna know my secret?"

"Yes."

He stood up and stepped closer to me, handing me three more potatoes to hold. I juggled them in my arms as he moved his mouth next to my ear and spoke softly.

"I have *really* good manners."

We sat at the table behind the cottage and peeled the potatoes into a pot of cold water. The family only had one potato peeler, which Jonty had chivalrously handed to me while taking possession of a paring knife. But it quickly transpired that I was the one who'd been given the raw end of the deal.

"This is the bluntest peeler in the world," I told him in frustration as it skimmed over the surface of the potato without even making a mark. "It doesn't even get the dirt off, let alone the skin."

Jonty just grinned as he deftly peeled his own spud, then tossed it into the pot with a flick of his wrist. "You want the knife?" He flipped it around in his hand and held it out to me, handle first. I looked at it suspiciously.

"I'd probably just cut my fingers off."

Jonty spun the knife back around and grasped the handle again. "Wouldn't want that."

"You just want to watch me struggle," I told him petulantly, making another valiant attempt to peel the potato. "I'd have better luck doing this with a spoon."

"A good workman never blames his equipment," Jonty told me, then grinned as I stuck my tongue out at him. "Just leave it, I'll do it in a sec."

"You know the most nutritious part of a potato is its skin," I said, setting the peeler down and rolling the potato across the table towards him. "You're actually denying yourself essential nutrients by taking it off."

"But then what would Murray eat?" he asked, flicking potato peelings onto the grass behind him, where the goat was scoffing them up greedily. "You want him to starve?"

I smiled at him, resting my chin on my hand and staring around. Phoebe was sitting on the tyre swing by the back fence, her legs stuck straight out in front of her with pointed toes as she swung around and around in haphazard circles. She was singing to herself, lost in her own world, and I watched her for a while, trying to remember what it was like to be so carefree.

Morgan, Jonty's second-youngest sister, was sitting cross-legged on the corrugated iron roof of Murray's little hut with her nose buried in a dog-eared paperback. I tilted my head, trying to catch a glimpse at what she was reading.

"*The Outsiders.*"

I turned to look at Jonty, and he raised his eyebrows speculatively.

"How can you tell?" I asked, trying to get a look at the cover from where I was sitting.

"It's her favourite. She reads it constantly. Gets to the end and then just starts over again at the beginning. Right Morgan?"

His sister lifted one hand away from the book and flipped him the bird. Jonty grinned at her and picked up the last potato off the table, unperturbed.

"Guess I got *all* the manners in this family."

"Well it's a good book," I said in Morgan's defence. "I must've read it at least ten times myself."

She lifted her head, eyes lighting up at my words. "Really?" I nodded, and she shut the book and jumped off the goat's hut, coming towards us.

"Now you've started it," Jonty muttered. "She'll chew your ear off about that book for hours."

"Good." I smiled at Morgan as she sat down next to me, her hands clasped over the tattered paperback. "Have you read any of her other books?"

Morgan frowned, seeming confused. "Her?"

"Yeah. S.E. Hinton, the author, has written a few other books as

35

well. You should read *Tex*," I told her. "That's my favourite. Well, my second favourite, after that one."

A flicker of a smile crossed Morgan's face, then she stared down at the book in her hands. "I didn't even know a woman wrote this."

"A girl, really," I said. "She wrote it when she was in high school, and it was published when she was only seventeen." The incredulous look on Morgan's face made me smile. "True story. I did a school project on her last year."

"Nerd," Jonty muttered under his breath.

I knew he was teasing, but I saw the way that Morgan's face shuttered at the word, and I straightened up and looked across the table at him defiantly.

"I like reading. You got a problem with that?"

From the corner of my eye I saw Morgan sit up a little taller, giving her brother an equally determined look. Jonty raised his hands in a gesture of surrender.

"No problem. You're both smarter than me, I get it."

"Too right we are." I turned back to Morgan and looked affectionately at the novel in her hands. "I've got the rest of her books at home. I'll lend them to you, if you want."

Morgan's face lit up. "Really? You'd do that?"

"Of course. I'll give one to Jonty tomorrow to pass along to you."

Morgan gave her brother a suspicious look as he stood up, lifting the pot of peeled potatoes with one hand and placing the other over his heart. "And I promise to faithfully deliver it, if you promise not to talk about it non-stop for the next six years."

"Don't ask people to make promises they can't keep," I told him as he walked behind me on his way to the house. Jonty dropped a hand onto my shoulder and kissed the top of my head as he passed, making me blush.

"He really likes you," Morgan said softly, opening *The Outsiders* again and smoothing her hand lovingly across the page.

"I really like him too," I admitted to her. "You got pretty lucky with your family."

I'd been expecting her to smile, but Morgan just shrugged, her face going blank. "They're okay I guess."

She hunched her shoulders over, her long hair obscuring her face as she focused on the book she was holding. I looked over at Phoebe, who was now hanging upside down with her legs hooked through the tyre, her outstretched fingers lightly brushing the grass. The back door banged shut, and I turned to see Jonty coming back out of the house, now accompanied by Bella. She looked equal parts pleased and embarrassed to see me, but she greeted me with a shy smile.

"Jonty said you're staying for dinner."

"Uh..." I shot him a look, to which he just smiled, straddling the bench seat next to me and scooting in close. He slid an arm around my waist, rested his chin on my shoulder and whispered in my ear.

"Please."

"Stop it," I told him, trying to be firm, but he just winked at me. I sighed and shook my head at Bella. "How do you live with this, day in and day out?"

She shrugged. "We struggle through."

Jonty sat up straighter, his fingers gently rubbing up and down my spine. "So you're gonna stay?"

I bit my lip, unsure. I wanted to. I liked spending time with them, liked how sweet and friendly his sisters were, but I also knew that they didn't have much to go around. Yet there seemed to be no good way to say no without offending them, and as I glanced from Bella's hopeful face to Morgan's eyes peeking anxiously through the thick curtain of her dark hair, I knew I'd been cornered.

"Sure. If it's okay with your mum."

Jonty stood up, grinning as he grabbed my hand. "Let's go ask her."

I wanted to refuse, but there was no polite way to do that, so I reluctantly let him pull me to my feet, and walked with him to the back door.

Jonty pulled it open and motioned me through. "After you."

I stepped into the cottage, looking around. I hadn't been in here in years, not since I was little. Hayley and I had played down here a few times when we were small, making up stories and pretending that we lived here. We'd acted out our favourite stories – Goldilocks and the Three Bears, eating imaginary porridge; Sleeping Beauty, being raised in the cottage by her fairy godmothers; Little Red Riding Hood, on her way to her grandmother's house. *All the better to see you with, my dear.* The cottage had looked different in my imagination every time, but had never looked quite like this.

The walls had no internal cladding, and creepers were growing in around the windows. My eyes darted around the room, cataloguing the scant furniture. An old yellow couch with a pillow and pile of neatly folded blankets at one end. A tatty standard lamp with a paisley shade, a small TV sitting on an old wooden trunk, a coffee table covered in someone's homework. A single light bulb dangling over the top of a small, rickety dining table with mismatched chairs pushed up against it. A rust-speckled fridge humming noisily in the corner. Crockery resting on shelves made from plywood and cinder blocks next to a stove top with two burners missing. A row of potted herbs growing merrily on the windowsill.

If you'd asked me what I'd expected, I don't know what I would've said, but it wasn't this. I knew they struggled, I knew they didn't have much – hell, I knew they lived in this falling-down little shack, but somehow I'd never realised that things were quite this bad. I hoped my shock wasn't showing on my face as Jonty came into the cottage behind me.

"Mum?"

I took a breath, trying desperately to seem nonchalant as Jonty's mother appeared in the doorway of one of the adjacent rooms. There were two bedrooms, I remembered, with a tiny bathroom between them. That was it. I thought of our big, sprawling homestead, with its state-of-the-art kitchen appliances, of our two lounges, of my own generously sized bedroom. How did six people live in this tiny space without driving each other mad?

Jonty's mother looked deeply alarmed to see me inside the house. Jonty stepped in closer to me and put an arm around my waist. I think he meant it to be comforting, but it only made me feel even more awkward.

"Tess can stay for dinner, right?"

She forced herself to smile. "Of course, if she'd like to. We're not having anything flash," she added, glancing in my direction. "But you're more than welcome."

"Thanks." I bit my lip, trying to resist the urge to peer into her bedroom, wondering what it was like. The house was tidy, at least, and as clean as it could be. She obviously took good care of it, but my heart ached for her. It had been four years, I reminded myself. Surely whatever the circumstances had been that got them into this mess could've got them out of it by now?

Jonty's mother walked past us and over to the stove, where she lifted the lid on the bubbling potatoes and peered at them. "How're things going on the farm, Tess?"

"Good thanks." I could feel my skin burning, and I stumbled over my words. "Busy, of course. As always. At this time of year."

She looked over her shoulder at me. "Is it? I'm afraid I don't know much about farming. Even after living here all these…"

She reddened as well, and I wished I could just suck all of the awkwardness out of the room. Jonty, for his part, didn't seem to be feeling it. He was sitting backwards on one of the mismatched chairs, watching us as though we were having a meaningful conversation instead of stumbling and dancing around each other's well-meaning words.

"We're bringing all the hoggets in this weekend," I explained.

"Drenching and vaxxing, and they've got to be weighed to find out whether they're big enough to go to the ram."

"What's a hogget?"

I looked over at the doorway, where Phoebe was standing, rocking back and forth on the balls of her feet.

"Um, last year's lambs. They're about eight months old now."

Her eyebrows shot up in an exact mimicry of the way her brother's did, which made me smile. "Are you going to eat them?"

"No, we're going to breed from them."

I watched Phoebe's forehead crease. "Aren't they too young to have babies?"

"Teen pregnancies are everywhere," I told her. "Especially on farms."

She pulled a face as her mother smiled.

"And if they don't make weight?"

I wasn't sure if she was actually interested, or just being polite, but I answered her. "They get sold."

"Or you eat them," Phoebe insisted.

"Sometimes."

"Sounds like you've got a busy weekend ahead," Jonty's mum said. "If you need any extra hands, Nate will be around. He's always happy to help out where he can. We'd like to make ourselves useful."

She sounded anxious, so I nodded. "Okay, thanks. I'll tell Dad."

I wasn't sure what my father's response would be. He didn't like Nate Fisher very much, and he hadn't called him up for stock work in a while. But although Bayard had left school and was working on the farm full-time now, one of the other hands was back at university for the semester and another was laid up with a back injury, so we were admittedly short-staffed.

"I'll help too, if you can use me," Jonty said.

"Always."

He smiled at me as his mother pulled some meat out of the

refrigerator and slapped it onto the bench. Phoebe started humming again, a tune I thought I knew but couldn't quite place.

Outside the cottage, a car came up the road, its engine not quite loud enough to drown out the heavy rock music blasting from its tinny speakers. I frowned, turning my head towards the sound of tyres skidding to a stop on the gravel.

Phoebe quit humming, and when I turned back to look at her, she'd disappeared. The tension that had finally dissipated out of the room was back in full force, and I looked from Jonty to his mother, trying to work out what was happening. A car door slammed, and someone said something. Jonty stood up and took hold of my hand, linking his fingers through mine. I could feel his palms sweating, and instinctively moved closer to him.

The front door swung open, and his father walked into the house. His eyes landed straight on me, and I sensed Jonty's tension, even as he tried to seem relaxed.

"Hello, what've we got here? A visitor from the big house?" Nate came towards me, his smile not quite reaching his eyes.

Jonty spoke before I could. "Tess just stopped by to meet Murray." His tone was light and jovial as he smiled at his father, but he never loosened his grip on my hand.

"Is that right?" Nate pulled a pack of cigarettes out of his pocket and tapped one into his palm. Nobody said anything as he pulled out a lighter and lit it, then took a deep drag. "What'd you think?"

I struggled to think of what to say to that. "Um, he's nice."

Nate exhaled, letting out a long stream of smoke. I blinked, trying not to get it in my eyes.

"Nice, is he?" He looked from me to Jonty, then back again with an amused expression. "Nice," he repeated, and I felt my cheeks burning.

Jonty's thumb stroked the back of my hand. "Tess was just heading home."

"Of course she was. Wouldn't want to be late for dinner," Nate said, taking another drag on his cigarette as he looked over at the meal his wife was preparing. "Unless you want to stay and eat with us."

He knew I'd refuse. Part of me wanted to accept, just to see the look on his face, but even as I entertained the notion, I was already shaking my head.

"No thanks. Maybe another time."

Nate just shrugged as Jonty led me past his father and out the front door. We were a hundred metres or so down the road, our hands still tightly clasped, when Jonty finally spoke.

"Sorry about that."

"It's okay." I looked at him sideways, but he wouldn't meet my eyes. "Is he always like that?"

"Like what?"

I shrugged, lacking words for what had happened. "I don't know. That."

Jonty frowned, kicking a stone out of his path. "I dunno. I guess. Some days are better than others. Can we not talk about him?"

"Okay. What d'you wanna talk about?"

He shrugged. "We don't have to talk."

I stopped, incredulous. If there was one thing Jonty rarely stopped doing, it was talking. "Who are you, and what've you done with my boyfriend?"

Jonty's face relaxed into his familiar crooked smile, and he flicked the hair out of his eyes as he stepped in closer to me. "Shh." He leaned in and kissed me softly on the lips. "I said no talking."

"You're not the boss of me," I mumbled, in between kisses, and he laughed.

"I know. But I can pretend."

4

FATHERS

The hot midday sun was beating down on the back of my head as I sat on the fence in the stockyards, holding the handle of the drafting gate and waiting. Dad released another hogget from the weigh crate, and the young sheep ran across the hard-packed dirt, her eyes fixed on the open gateway ahead of her, relieved that her ordeal was over. By the time she got to me, she'd been driven up into the race by Jock and the dogs to where Gordy was weaving his way through the tightly-packed sheep with a drenching backpack, tipping the hoggets' heads back and squirting a dose into each one's mouth. The sheep were then shuttled forward into another narrow pen where Hugh was administering vaccinations against campylobacter, before Bayard pushed them into the weigh crate one at a time for Dad.

Jonty's father Nate had turned up at the yards this morning to offer his assistance, and had been assigned to help Hugh by penning and holding sheep for their vaccinations. The hoggets, being young, hadn't been through the yards much and could be a bit of a handful. I was disappointed that Jonty hadn't been with him, but hadn't had a chance to find out why.

A rivulet of sweat ran down my spine as the weigh crate gates clanked shut behind the next hogget, and Dad shaded the electronic scale with one hand, squinting at the output on its screen. I could tell from the way he shook his head as he jotted the weight down on the clipboard that this one hadn't made the grade, and before he even said the words, I'd swung the drafting gate to the other side and let the hogget run into the left-hand yard.

"Send her left," Dad called without looking up, then nodded to me when he saw I'd pre-empted him.

The group of hoggets in the left-hand pen were less numerous than those on the right, but still made up an uncomfortable percentage of our stock. Far more than we wanted to be coming in underweight, but we were in the middle of a drought. Supplementary feed would be critical before they went to the ram in a couple of weeks' time, but if they were well underweight, they wouldn't be going to the ram at all. An underweight ewe was far less likely to have a successful conception and birth, and every animal around here was expected to pay their way.

"One-six-five," Bayard called up to Dad as he shut the weigh crate behind the next hogget, and my head spun back around to face it as I recognised the ear tag number.

Mildred. I crossed my fingers tightly as Dad looked at the output screen with a frown. Mildred and her twin sister Myrtle were bottle lambs that we'd hand-reared after their mother had died shortly after their birth. Fortunately we'd found them in time and had managed to pull them through. They'd turned into rambunctious little lambs, and had been integrated back into the mob months ago. Mildred had always been the bigger and stronger of the two, and I breathed a sigh of relief as Dad nodded approvingly and jotted her weight down on his clipboard.

"She's right."

He opened the gate and Mildred jogged out into the raceway. I called softly to her as she passed, but she ignored me, sprinting through the gate with a leap in the air for good measure. I was smiling after her when a commotion broke out further down the race, and all heads turned towards Hugh. He was shaking his head and yelling something at Nate. Dad frowned in their direction as a dust cloud rose up behind me, and our red farm ute bounced across the potholes and into the yard.

"Lunch is here," I told Dad, but he wasn't listening.

"What's going on over there?" he asked Bayard, who just shrugged as he let the next hogget onto the scales.

Dad leaned on the top of the crate and looked down the race. "There a problem?" he called.

Hugh turned towards him, pushing his cap back on his head. "They got let out early, and I'm pretty sure I missed a couple. No idea which ones," he said irritably, gesturing towards the swirling mob of sheep.

Dad swore loudly. "How'd that happen?"

Hugh looked pointedly at Nate, who threw his hands into the air and started trying to defend himself by insisting that Hugh had *told* him to open the gate. Hugh just shook his head in clear disagreement, and my heart sank, knowing what was coming.

My father never had any patience for people who tried to pass on the blame. You could get something wrong – mistakes happen, and he understood that – but my father had no time at all for anyone who got something wrong and then refused to own up to it, or worse, tried to blame someone else for their own mistake. Hugh had been working on our farm for almost as long as I'd been alive, and nothing in the world that Nate said now was going to get my father to take his word against Hugh's.

I closed my eyes and listened as the men shouted back and forth, then Dad's command cut through the commotion. We were breaking for lunch, and Nate was going home.

"Dad?"

My father turned towards me as he sipped hot tea from the mug in his hand. "Tess."

"Now that we're a man short…" I started, as Hugh snorted disparagingly.

"Half a man," he muttered bitterly. "A quarter, probably. One of the dogs could've done a better job."

Dad said nothing, just took another sip of his tea and waited. I swallowed hard and finished my sentence, knowing what kind of reaction I was going to get from Hugh.

"I could get Jonty to come up and replace him."

Hugh shook his head in disgust, as predicted. "What makes you think he'd be any more use than his old man?"

"Because he will be. I promise." I looked at Dad. "Will you give him a shot? Please?"

Dad mulled it over, his expression unreadable. "We *are* short-handed," he said eventually.

"Great," Hugh muttered. "Isn't this just my lucky day."

I said nothing, certain that Jonty would change Hugh's opinion of him if he was only given the chance. Dad squished a mozzie on the back of his neck, then nodded at me.

"If he can get here in the next fifteen minutes, I'll consider it."

"Done deal," I said quickly, immediately heading towards the ute. "I'll be right back!"

I jumped into the driver's seat, depressed the clutch and started the engine. I'd been driving the farm vehicles since I was about eleven years old, and I backed the ute easily and turned it around, then headed back up the road to collect Jonty. I passed Nate on the way, walking towards his house, but I didn't slow down. I was fairly certain that being replaced on the job by his son wasn't going to make Nate Fisher's day any better.

"One-six-four."

My attention snapped back to the weigh crate in front of me as Bayard shut the gate behind Myrtle. I'd been watching Jonty, who was helping Ollie move the sheep from the pen up into the race. Hugh had rejected him as a direct replacement for his father, insisting that he could do a better and faster job working without assistance, but the whole operation had slowed down noticeably since lunch.

Dad wrote something on his clipboard and pulled the lever to open the gate.

"Left."

My heart thudded in my chest as Myrtle trotted out of the crate and started to head towards the open gate, which was still letting into the right hand pen.

"Send her *left*, Tess!" Dad barked at me, and I swung the gate just in time, cutting Myrtle off. She stopped, then slowly turned her head towards the left-hand pen, but didn't move.

"Are you sure?" I asked Dad.

"She's well underweight." He looked at the chart again, then back at me. "Is this one of the bottle lambs?"

"She was Hayley's," I said, hoping for a reprieve even as I knew one would never come. There was no room for sentimentality on a farm. Especially one in the midst of a drought. But I had to try.

Dad frowned at me. "I don't remember Hayley feeding any lambs this season."

Well no, I wanted to say. *Of course you don't.* Hayley's interest in the lambs hadn't extended much beyond that first night, when we'd brought them up into the house, only hours old and soaking wet. But she'd been interested then - she'd named them, and had held Myrtle on her lap and tried to coax the limp lamb to suckle from a bottle while I'd wrapped my arms around Mildred's squirming body and done the same. For a few short hours, we'd revisited our childhood years spent raising bottle lambs, calling dibs on which one was 'ours' and arguing about whose was the cutest. Back when we were small, we'd spend hours with our bottle lambs, feeding them and fattening them up. We would teach them to follow us around, to walk on a lead and jump over obstacles; we'd taken them to lamb and calf days at school, and occasionally even shown them at our local A&P until show jumping had taken over our schedules. I didn't remind Dad that Hayley had lost interest after a few days, that I'd been the one getting up all through the night to feed the lambs while Hayley just patted them in passing. But if anything was going to soften my father up right now, it was the mention of Hayley.

"Can we just bring her home and fatten her up?" I pleaded. "You've still got time before tupping. I'm sure I could get more weight on her by then."

"Tess." Dad looked annoyed as Bayard shut the next hogget into the crate while Myrtle stayed in the middle of the race, looking up at me.

"Two-twenty-eight."

"Please, Dad?"

He looked back down at the scales and made another note on his clipboard, then pulled the gate open.

"Another one left," was all he said as the next hogget jumped down.

This little hogget ran straight for the open gateway, and Myrtle made her decision and followed, throwing a wee buck as she went. I watched her go, tears prickling the corners of my eyes.

"Fine, be like that," I told Dad. "But you have to tell Hayley that you're killing her pet."

Dad shaded the screen as he checked the weight of the next hogget.

"She's not a pet," he reminded me. "She's stock." He pulled the gate open and let the next hogget out, then nodded to me to move the drafting gate. "To the right."

I stabbed a long runner bean with my fork and glared at it as I sliced it in half.

"Jeez, Tess. What'd that bean ever do to you?"

I looked up to see Hayley watching me with an amused expression. I shrugged, aware that my parents' conversation about the market price of hoggets had abruptly ceased. These days, whenever Hayley said or did anything, the rest of the world stopped turning and paid attention to her.

"Nothing."

Dad loaded his fork with mashed potato, ignoring me. Mum just looked irritated and kept eating, glancing at Hayley every few seconds, presumably to make sure she was still there.

Hayley set her fork down and rested her chin on her hand.

"I call bullshit."

"Language, Hayley," Mum said half-heartedly, but my sister ignored her.

"Come on Tess, spit it out. If anyone's going to be moping around the dinner table, it should be the person who's going to have invasive brain surgery in a week." She gestured at herself with her thumb, ignoring Mum's gulp at the blatant reminder that her perfect daughter wasn't so perfect right now. "What's eating you?"

It sounded stupid, in the face of what she'd just reminded us. But I told her anyway.

"Dad's sending Myrtle to the sales," I said, staring straight into her bright blue eyes. "She didn't make weight, so…"

I drew a line across my throat and made choking noises, and Mum set down her cutlery with a clatter against the edge of her plate.

"Oh stop it, Tess," she snapped, but Hayley was looking at Dad with a stricken expression.

"Not really," she said to him, her eyes wide. "You're not really going to butcher little Myrtle, are you?"

Dad clenched his jaw and swallowed. "I'm not butchering anything. But she's not up to weight, so she's not going to the ram. And if I can't breed from her, there's no reason to keep her on the farm."

"But we can fatten her up," I insisted, and to her credit, Hayley nodded.

"Exactly. She had a rough start but she pulled through once, what makes you think she won't do it again?"

"What Hayley said," I agreed, smiling across the table at my sister. "If you just give her a chance, I'm sure she-"

"Hayley, we need to talk about your party."

My sister's head turned towards Mum, her attention caught, and I stared down at my plate, hopes sunk once again. If Hayley had fought for Myrtle, she might've had a chance at changing Dad's mind. But Mum had agreed to throw a party for Hayley before she went into hospital next week to remove the now-shrunken tumour in her brain, and what had started out as a small get-together of nearby family and close friends had turned into a major shindig, with half of Waipukurau on the invite list. We were holding it in the big woolshed, and Dad had only just managed to restrain Mum from hiring in caterers for the event, reminding her that there was nothing the locals liked more than to bring a plate of food to a pot luck meal.

"What about it?" Hayley asked, Myrtle's plight forgotten. "Have we worked out the sound system yet? Because Jenna knows a guy that we can hire one from, he'll come out and set it all up on the day, and she said it's not that expensive."

"Don't worry about the cost," Mum told her, ignoring Dad as he cleared his throat at the other end of the table. "This is your big night. Find out his number from Jenna, and I'll give him a call in the morning."

"How big exactly is this guest list?" Dad asked.

Hayley shrugged. "I don't know exact numbers. Tess hasn't told me yet how many people she's invited."

I blinked at her. "Me?"

Hayley tilted her head and smiled, but there was something in her eyes that I didn't trust. I wondered where she was going with all this.

"You have friends, don't you?"

I shrugged. "Um, well Jonty's coming."

Hayley laughed. "Duh. I figured that went without saying, seeing as how you two are basically joined at the hip these days. I heard he's even started helping on the farm now. Is that because he can't bear to be away from you, or because he wants a stake in your inheritance?" She raised her eyebrows speculatively. "Is he a gold digger?"

Dad snorted. "Not much gold around here," he muttered, choosing to ignore the rest of what Hayley had said. "He did all right today. Jock said he wasn't completely useless," he conceded, which was major praise, coming from him.

I smiled down at my dinner plate, but my satisfaction didn't last long.

"Unlike his father," Mum said, unable to resist the opportunity for a jibe. "Honestly John, we need to make a decision about that family."

"What decision?" I asked. "What's to decide?"

"They can't go on living in the cottage," Mum said. "It's not safe."

"Not now," Dad told her, but she bit back.

"You can't keep putting it off! That place is falling down around their ears. What happens when one of those children falls through a rotten floorboard, or a piece of roof iron falls off and cuts someone?" Mum set her cutlery down and jabbed her finger at him down the table. "It's our property, and *we* are the ones who'd be liable if anything happened. I talked to Marg about it last week, and she said that it could cost us thousands, maybe hundreds of thousands, in compensation."

"Don't be ridiculous," Dad scoffed.

"Have you read the law?" she demanded. "Because Marg has, and she knows it back to front. We need to get them out and tear the place down. It's barely standing as it is – one nudge and the whole structure would probably collapse."

"It's not *that* bad!" I argued quickly. "It looks worse from the outside than it really is. It's still solid, nobody's going to fall through the floor…"

Everyone's eyes were on me now, but it was Hayley who spoke first.

"So you *have* been inside," she said. "I knew it."

She grinned wolfishly at me, and I picked up my glass of milk and took a sip, stalling for time.

"Please tell me you're joking," Mum snapped.

My fingers tightened around the glass, and I stared across the table at my sister's plate of half-eaten food. The only thing on it that she'd touched was the mashed potato. Since the radiation treatment, her sense of taste had been all over the place. At first it had just been salty food that she couldn't stand, then it was anything sour or bitter, and lately she'd even gone off sweets. It was driving Mum crazy, watching her subsist on a bland diet of mashed potatoes and pasta. It wasn't the only side effect she was experiencing – she was often tired, sometimes confused, and occasionally spaced out completely. Unfortunately, however, none of the radiation seemed to have made her into a nicer person.

"Tess?" Mum pushed, but Dad interjected.

"I'll go down next week and do an inspection," he said. "Take a look for myself, make a decision based on that."

Mum pursed her lips but sat back, mollified – at least for the moment – as Hayley scooped up a forkful of potato and lifted it towards her mouth.

"So tell us, Tess," she said, raising an eyebrow speculatively. "What's Jonty's bed like? Comfy?"

I'd had enough. "Shut up!" I snapped, getting to my feet.

My sister met my eyes unflinchingly. "Make me."

I put one hand on the table, leaned forward, and poured my glass of milk onto her half-eaten meal. It spilled over the edges of the plate and onto the table, dripping into her lap. Mum started yelling at me as Hayley swiftly retaliated, grabbing a fistful of milk-soaked mashed potato and smeared it into my hair, gripping my ponytail to hold me in place. I dropped my glass, and it rolled off the table and smashed on the floor. Colin started barking in alarm on the front porch, scrabbling at the door to try and get in and come to my rescue, and Dad banged on the table with his fist.

"Cut it out!"

Hayley let go of me and we separated, white-hot rage burning between us. Mum was on her feet, hurrying to Hayley's side, taking her part as always because she was the favourite child, the invalid, the one that Mum cared most about. I'd always known that, deep down, but lately it was as though she couldn't even be bothered trying to hide it. I sat back down in my chair, my scalp burning, and started picking the potato out of my hair with one hand as I picked up my fork to finish my meal.

But Mum wasn't having that.

"Tess, go to your room right now. And stay there."

I walked down the dirt road as quickly as I could, clutching the long rope tightly in my hand. Colin bounded ahead, his pale coat gleaming in the light of the full moon. It was a beautiful night, the sky above as black as pitch and speckled with endless stars. Colin stopped and looked impatiently back at us, and I picked up my pace, tugging at the end of the rope. Myrtle broke into a jog alongside me, her cloven hooves tapping softly on the road. My dog barked, telling us to hurry up, and I raised a finger to my lips.

"Shh!" I warned him. He lowered his pointed ears and drooped his tail, ashamed of being reprimanded. I caught up to him and rubbed his head apologetically. "Stay quiet, Colin. This is a rescue mission."

Colin wagged his tail, pretending to understand. He didn't care why we were out walking in the middle of the night. He was just happy to be on an adventure.

The dark cottage emerged gradually out of the shadows up ahead, and my steps faltered as I wondered if I was doing the right thing. Myrtle dropped her head and tugged me towards the grass on the side of the road for a midnight snack. I let her eat a few mouthfuls, then took a deep breath, pulled her head up and led her on.

My boots crunched on the gravel as I walked her around the side of the house towards Murray's little corrugated iron lean-to. The hedge along the front boundary meant that the goat hut wasn't visible from the road – not unless you were looking really hard when you went past – and it would be the best place to hide Myrtle.

It was the only place I could think of.

Murray heard us coming and jumped on top of his hut with a clatter, bleating furiously, like some kind of goat-watchdog-hybrid. Colin unhelpfully barked at him, and I hissed furiously at him to shut up. He obeyed, but Myrtle and Murray weren't so well-trained, and started bleating back at each other.

"Shh!"

I tied the long rope to the fence behind Murray's lean-to, and Myrtle promptly stopped yelling and started grazing. Murray kept at it, but I wasn't worried about him. If he woke anyone up, they'd just think he was yelling at the moon or something. Relieved, I turned around and started walking slowly back towards the road when I realised that my dog was missing.

"Colin?" I whispered.

I was about to risk a low whistle when I spotted him, his pale coat evident in the bright moonlight. He had his forefeet on the front step of the cottage and was staring adoringly up at Jonty, who was leaning against the door frame and watching me.

Busted.

I lifted a hand and waved, and Jonty stepped out of the house, closing the door carefully behind him. Colin trailed devotedly at his heels as Jonty walked past me and looked down the side of the house to where Myrtle was clearly visible, still peacefully grazing while Murray strained at the end of his chain in an attempt to reach her.

"What are you doing, Tess?"

"I had to save her! I couldn't let Dad send her off to the sales."

Jonty ran a hand through his hair, rumpling it back and forth. "But you can't bring her here."

"Where am I supposed to take her?"

My voice was getting louder, and he took me by the arm and led me away from the house, back towards the road. Colin trotted along ahead of us, his tail wagging back and forth rhythmically. At least he was enjoying himself.

"I had to do *something*, Jonty."

"If your old man finds out she's here…"

"He won't."

"…he'll accuse us of stealing. You do know that, right?"

"I'll tell him the truth."

"When? After we've been found out?"

I shook my head. "Tomorrow morning, once the others have gone to the sales. They're taking them first thing in the morning, Jonty, before it gets light. It was now or never to rescue her."

He wasn't convinced. "And you think he won't notice that he's got a sheep missing?"

"I changed the count last night," I told him. "He left his clipboard on his desk, and I turned the six into a five. He's got messy writing anyway, he struggles to read it at the best of times."

Jonty was still angry. "And what if I hadn't heard you? Was I just supposed to wake up and find a sheep in the garden and think nothing of it?"

"I don't *know*," I told him, losing the battle to fight back tears. "I didn't know what else to do, okay? I just had to save her. I couldn't let her die." I wiped my face with my sleeve, and Jonty relented, putting

55

his arms around me and pulled me in for a hug. I rested my cheek against his shoulder. His skin was warm and he smelled like cheap soap. "I can't just let her die."

Jonty took a slow, deep breath. "I know. It's just…"

I nodded, understanding. I pulled back from his embrace, wiping my eyes again. "It was stupid. I shouldn't have brought her here. I'll take her away, find somewhere else."

He bit his lip, and looked in the direction of Myrtle, hidden now behind the overgrown hedge.

"You can leave her here for now. As long as you promise to tell your dad, first thing in the morning. Maybe if he realises how desperate you are, he'll change his mind, let you keep her and fatten her up."

I sniffed. "You think so?"

"Worth a shot, isn't it?" he said with a shrug. I nodded, and he pulled me towards him and kissed my forehead. "Come on. I'll walk you home."

5

FIRING LINE

When I woke the next morning, sunlight was streaming through the crack in my bedroom curtains. I lay there blinking, chasing the remnants of a swiftly vanishing dream. Colin padded into my room and pushed his nose into my hand. I scruffed his head and smiled at him.

"You're not supposed to be in here," I told him. "Bad dog." He wagged his tail, tongue hanging out the side of his mouth as he panted in my face. "And your breath is terrible."

Colin didn't care. He put his front paws up onto the bed and licked my face.

"Ugh, seriously! What'd I just say?" I asked him, pushing him away half-heartedly. He buried his muzzle into the blankets and stared at me with sad puppy eyes, making me laugh. My bed was soft and warm, and I had no immediate desire to get out of it. "Come on then," I told him, patting the blankets next to me. Colin jumped onto the bed and lay across my legs, his tail thumping happily against the mattress.

Someone outside blew a dog whistle, and Colin sat up again, his large pointed ears sticking up comically. Sheep were bleating nearby in a loud chorus, drowned out only momentarily by the familiar revving of a quad bike. I heard it pass the house with a clatter that could only be an empty stock trailer being towed along behind, bouncing over the potholes as it traversed them at speed.

I looked over at my alarm clock, wondering what time it was, then sat bolt upright. It was almost eight, and reality came flooding back as the pieces of the puzzle fell together. Hoggets. Sales. Stock truck.

Myrtle.

Jonty.

I leapt out of bed and ran to the window, yanking the curtains back and staring at Bayard's familiar back as he drove away on the quad. Without stopping to get dressed, I ran down the hall and through the kitchen. Mum was sitting at the table going over some paperwork, and she jumped in surprise as I came racing past with Colin on my heels, his nails skidding on the polished floorboards as we rounded the corner

"Tess, where are you going? And *what* is that dog doing in my house?"

I ignored her as I ran out onto the porch and shoved my feet into my boots as quickly as I could. Colin leapt onto the lawn and waited for me eagerly, then took off like a mottled streak towards the yards, with me puffing in his wake.

Dad was standing up at the yards with his clipboard, frowning at it while two of the farmhands stood nearby and watched him. They all looked up as I ran towards them, coming to a puffing halt at the gate.

"Dad, can I talk to you?"

He set his clipboard down on the top railing of the yards and crossed his arms. "Go right ahead. Maybe you'd like to start by explaining why one of my hoggets is missing."

I glanced at the other farmhands, suddenly very aware that I was standing there barefoot and braless in an old purple Horse of the Year t-shirt and faded pyjama shorts with apples on them.

I blinked, feigning innocence. "Is – is there?"

"Don't play games with me Tess," Dad said, pinning me with a steely glare. "The way I see this is there are two possible situations right now. Either you know where she is," he paused for emphasis, slowly raising an eyebrow, "or you don't."

"I…" I hung my head, unable to look him in the face any longer. So much for saving a life today. "I know where she is."

"Good. So do I."

I looked back up at him. "You do?"

"Bayard spotted her on the way in this morning."

"Oh." *How on earth had he managed that?* I swallowed hard. "I was going to tell you first thing, only I slept in." He looked unimpressed. "I just wanted her to have another chance."

"So you stole her."

"Well no, I just moved her. Technically she's still on your property."

Dad just glared at me, unamused. "Whose idea was it?"

"Mine," I said quickly. "Jonty knew nothing about it until I turned up there last night."

"And if he had any sense, he'd have told you to turn around and take her straight home," Dad grumbled. "But he let her stay, which makes him just as much to blame as you in this. More, since she's *not* his property."

"Please don't blame him!" I said quickly. "He was really mad at me, but I was desperate." I brushed at the tears escaping from the corners of my eyes, and Dad looked uncomfortable. He didn't like it when people cried.

"Women," he muttered. "Get in the ute. Now."

We didn't speak as we drove down the road towards Jonty's house. Bayard had the quad parked on the side of the road when we arrived, the trailer gate open and the ramp down, and Jonty was standing next to it, talking to Bayard with a pleading expression. I felt the hairs on my arms stand up as Nate came marching down the path from the house, pointing in Myrtle's direction and yelling something at Jonty, who hunched his shoulders but said nothing. Dad pulled up behind the quad, and I leapt down from the cab and started towards Jonty. He glanced at me with a wary expression and shook his head slightly, making me stop in my tracks. Behind him I could see Morgan sitting on the front steps of their house, her knees pulled up to her chin and her arms wrapped tightly around herself.

Nate turned towards Dad as he approached him, opening his hands away from his body in a gesture of surrender.

"I know why you're here but trust me, we had nothing to do with that sheep turning up on our lawn." He glared at me. "It's that girl of yours, setting us up. I don't know what she thinks she's playing at, but…"

Dad stopped in front of him. He was almost a foot taller than Nate, who didn't look like he'd shaved – or showered – in several days. He smelled strongly of stale beer and cigarettes, and out of the corner of my eye, I caught the disgusted look that Bayard was giving him.

"Let me deal with Tess. For now I just want my sheep back."

"I'll get her," Jonty offered, turning on his heel and heading towards Myrtle, who was grazing alongside the pot-bellied goat.

"I swear I knew nothing about it, not until about five minutes ago." Nate glared at his son's retreating back, and shook his head. "I'll deal with Jonty, don't you worry about that. I'll make sure he knows he did wrong."

"He's okay," Dad said calmly. "Tess told me what happened, and I don't blame Jonty for any part that he had in this. But in future, I'd appreciate it if you ring me straightaway when you find any of my stock in a place that they shouldn't be."

Nate assured Dad that he would as Jonty led Myrtle back across the lawn and held out the rope towards Dad. He nodded his head towards Bayard, who took her from Jonty and led her up to the trailer, grabbed her around the middle and lifted her into it. There was a clatter as Murray jumped onto his hut and bleated a pitiful farewell. Bayard shut the gate behind the hogget with a clank and latched it securely.

"Right. Well, no harm done." Dad nodded to Bay, who climbed back onto the quad and started the engine. "Sorry for the inconvenience," he told Nate, who huffed as he turned back towards the house.

Morgan scrambled to her feet as he approached and quickly disappeared inside, but Jonty stayed where he was, eyes downcast.

Dad turned and started walking back to the driver's door of the ute. "C'mon Tess. Oh, and Jonty?" Jonty looked up quickly, his expression wary. "In future, when my daughter comes to you with one of her hare-brained schemes, at least *try* and talk her out of it."

A smile flickered across Jonty's face as he nodded. "I can do that."

"I don't rate your chances, to be honest," Dad said, shooting me a look as he walked back to the ute. "She's bloody stubborn when she wants to be. Gets it from her mother, of course."

I grinned at him as I followed. He pulled the driver's door open and started to get in, then paused, one foot in the vehicle and one on the road as he looked at Jonty.

"One more thing."

Jonty looked nervous. "Yeah?"

Dad drummed his fingers on the roof of the cab as I braced myself for him to deliver the inspection notice that he'd promised Mum last night. I wondered how long he'd give the Fishers to get the place into decent shape, and whether they had a hope in hell of pulling it off. But Dad surprised me.

"We could use some more help with the stock today," Dad said. "You free?"

Jonty stared at him. "Really? I mean yeah. Yeah, of course I am. Definitely." He broke into a bright smile, and I felt my heart lift at his obvious excitement. "Uh…right now?"

Dad nodded. "Yeah." He motioned to the tray of the ute, and

Jonty moved quickly towards it. "Jump in."

My father settled into the driver's seat and shut the door with a clank as Jonty ran towards the house to get his boots. Dad looked across at me, taking in the wide grin on my face, and shook his head.

"Only 'cos we're short staffed," he reminded me.

"Uh huh," I said, pretending to accept his reasoning.

He narrowed his eyes slightly but started the engine without further comment. Jonty ran back over to us and scrambled into the tray, his boots clutched in one hand.

Dad put the ute into first and checked his wing mirror reflexively. "You really think you can get that hogget fattened up before the ram goes out?"

My heart jolted in my chest. "Yes! Definitely."

"Well then." Dad released the clutch as he drove forward, eyes on the road. "Guess I'd better give her another shot after all."

6

FIX YOU

I woke up the next morning to the unmistakeable smell of burning. Swiftly kicking off my blankets, I hurried barefoot down the hallway, following my nose towards the kitchen. I could hear my mother swearing and dropping pans into the sink, and I pushed the door open to see her through a gauzy haze of smoke.

"Are you trying to burn the house down?" I asked her, coughing a little as I walked over to the window above the sink and opened it wider. "Because a little warning would've been nice."

"I was making pancakes," Mum said thickly, dumping a sizzling frying pan in the sink and running water over it. She sniffed as she stared at the steamed-up window, then rubbed her eyes with the sleeve of her dressing gown. "For Hayley."

"Will she eat pancakes?" I asked dubiously, backtracking towards the front door and throwing it wide open.

"I don't know," Mum grumbled. She pulled the frying pan out of the sink and set it on the draining board. "She liked them before." She threw her hands up in a helpless gesture, then wiped her eyes again as I belatedly realised that it wasn't just the smoke that was making them water.

"Do you want some help?" I offered, stepping up to the kitchen bench and looking at the mess she'd made.

The bench surface was covered in flour and broken eggshells, and an unappetising pile of charred pancakes sat on a large plate next to a bowl of uncooked batter. I picked it up and looked inside. Clumps of flour bobbed to the top of the mixture, and I glanced back over at my mother dubiously. This looked more like something Dad had tried to make. Mum was usually a good cook, but this whole pancake situation was an unmitigated disaster.

"What's going on in here?"

We both turned at the sound of Hayley's voice. She walked into the room, looking around in confusion. "Is there a fire?"

"Mum was just burning you some pancakes," I told her. "You hungry?"

Hayley shrugged. She blinked several times, her eyes vague. "What's going on in here?" she repeated.

"Nothing, sweetheart," Mum said quickly, straightening up and going to Hayley's side. "Why don't you go and get dressed while Tess makes us some pancakes? Do you want bacon with yours?"

Hayley shook her head. "I don't…no. Yuck. I hate bacon."

She pulled a face, and I turned my head to catch my mother's stricken expression. Hayley loved bacon almost as much as she loved Misty, and I was pretty sure that the words *I hate bacon* had never crossed her lips before in her life.

"Okay then," Mum said, with forced cheer in her voice. "No bacon. Tess?"

"On it," I assured her.

I waited for them to leave the room before I tipped the lumpy pancake batter out into the sink. The sludgy yellow mixture swirled in the bottom of the sink, slowly making its way down the drain as I picked up the stack of charred pancakes and hurled it out of the kitchen window onto the lawn. Colin immediately bounded off the porch towards the discarded food, his tail held high and ears pricked.

"Oy! Leave it," I yelled at him. His pointed ears drooped and he turned to look at me sadly. "Don't make that face. You'd be sick if you ate all that."

A sparrow flew down behind him and hopped towards the pancakes. Colin gave the bird an agonised look before slinking back to the porch and heaving himself up the steps with a martyred sigh.

"You can thank me later," I told my dog, who thumped his tail once against the wooden porch as he lay down.

I measured flour into the bowl, keeping one eye on Colin as several more sparrows flitted down to see what was on offer, but they were promptly chased off by a pair of blackbirds who started squabbling over the scraps. My dog lowered his chin onto his paws and watched the birds moodily.

I had just started pouring fresh batter into the frying pan when Hayley came back into the room, still in her pyjamas.

"What're you doing?"

"Making pancakes," I told her, forcing myself to keep my voice light.

She woke up disoriented some mornings, almost as though she had trouble coming back to herself after sleep. It wore off quickly, but it was distressing to witness. I never thought I'd look forward to her merciless teasing, but there was something unnerving about how quiet she was right now, sitting at the kitchen table and staring blankly at Dad's discarded newspaper.

I flipped the pancake over as Mum reappeared, fully dressed with lipstick applied.

"Going somewhere?" I asked her curiously, trying to divert her attention from Hayley's vacant stare.

"I've got to pop into town this morning and pick up a few things," she said, her eyes fixed on my sister. "Then we've got an appointment with the oncologist this afternoon."

She walked over to my sister and put a hand on her forehead, as though checking whether she was running a temperature. It was an instinctive gesture that was sadly futile. What was wrong with my sister wasn't something she could diagnose, or fix. Hayley flinched away from her touch, then scowled up at her.

"I'm fine," she snapped. "Go away."

"We're seeing the doctor again this afternoon," Mum told her gently.

"I know, I heard you the first time."

I slid a golden pancake onto a plate and took it over to Hayley, then handed her a knife and fork. Mum hovered nearby, watching intently as Hayley picked up the utensils and cut into the pancake. She ate one mouthful, then another as I returned to the stove and poured out more batter.

"How is it?" Mum asked her anxiously.

"It's fine. Aren't you late for whatever it is you're rushing off to do?" Hayley asked, the food seemingly helping to restore her to her usual snarky self.

Mum glanced at her watch. "I've got a few minutes."

"Just go," my sister told her. "You're stressing me out, hovering around like that. Go on, piss off."

If Hayley wasn't sick, Mum would've never let her talk to her that way. I braced myself for a sharp retaliation, but Mum didn't say anything. She just walked out of the house, leaving the front door wide open behind her. Colin lifted his head off his paws and watched her go, then shuffled to the door and lay down on the doormat, peeking inside the house to surreptitiously watch me.

I flipped the next pancake over and glanced over at my sister's plate. Half of hers was gone, and she was still eating. My stomach rumbled, but I ignored it, keeping an eye on Hayley as she polished off the remainder of her pancake.

"Another?"

"Sure." Hayley smiled at me as I flipped it onto her plate. "You make good pancakes, T."

"Thanks, H."

Colin suddenly started barking, his claws scrabbling on the porch as he jumped to his feet.

"When are you going to train that dog?" Hayley asked me, lifting an eyebrow as we heard Colin leap off the porch, still barking.

"He's trained," I replied defensively. "He's a guard dog, listen to him."

"Uh huh. He sounds real threatening."

Colin's barks had ceased already, and I looked through the kitchen window to see him standing on his hind legs with his front paws up on Jonty's shoulders, enthusiastically licking my boyfriend's face.

"Invite him in." I turned to look at my sister. "It's Jonty, right?" Off my nod, she took another bite of pancake, then spoke around it. "I could tell by the look on your face. You're totally smitten. It's kinda gross."

"You're gross." It was a reflexive response, but it made Hayley grin.

"So invite him in. Mum's not here, and I won't tell."

I wasn't sure I believed her, but it wasn't like there was a rule against it. And I'd been inside his house, after all. I caught his eye and motioned to him through the window, and he came towards the house. I poured more batter into the frying pan as Hayley set down her knife and fork with a clatter.

"I'm full," she declared abruptly.

She'd only eaten half of her second pancake, but that was a pretty good effort for her lately. The drugs that made her feel queasy and affected her taste buds had seriously altered her formerly rampant appetite, and as a result she'd lost quite a bit of weight. While she jokingly referred to herself as 'bikini ready', I knew that our parents were concerned. Hayley stood up as Jonty appeared at the open front door, poking his head in.

"Morning. Hey, Hayley. How's it going?"

She stretched her arms over her head, revealing her smooth, flat stomach. "Morning." She lowered her arms and smiled enticingly.

"D'you like pancakes?"

Moments later Jonty was seated at the kitchen table, finishing off Hayley's breakfast.

"So are you riding Copper today?" she asked him, pouring milk into the mug of tea I'd just made her.

He nodded, and swallowed his mouthful of food. "That's why I'm here."

"Don't tell Tess," Hayley replied. "She'll be heartbroken to realise she's playing second fiddle to a horse."

"Nah." Jonty looked over at me, then winked. "She already knows."

Hayley laughed. "Are you going with him?"

I turned to face her. "Me?"

"No, I was talking to Colin." The dog raised his head at the sound of his name, his big pointed ears pricked up. "Yes, of course you. Are you riding today?"

"Um." I turned back to the stove, waiting for bubbles to form in the middle of the pancake batter. "Yeah." My stomach churned at the thought of it, but I knew I had to get back in the saddle. Not Misty's though. Not yet. "I'm bringing Rory back into work."

I waited for Hayley to argue, but it didn't happen. "Makes sense." She picked up her mug of tea and sipped it. "Probably less likely to buck you off."

At least she was being honest.

"Ah, bugger."

I looked over at Jonty, who was holding up Copper's left foreleg and looking at his hoof.

"What's wrong?"

"He's pulled a shoe."

I dropped Rory's leadrope and walked back towards Jonty, who was holding Copper in the middle of the five-acre paddock. The big chestnut horse dropped his nose to sniff Jonty's hip inquisitively.

"Great." I looked around as Jonty set Copper's hoof down. "Now we've got to find it."

"You ever consider training your dog to find lost horseshoes?" Jonty asked as Colin bounded past him in pursuit of a rabbit. It disappeared down a rabbit hole, and Colin skidded to a stop, then shoved his nose down the hole.

"Colin won't even fetch a tennis ball," I told him wryly. "I can't imagine him spending hours seeking out a cast shoe."

Jonty shrugged. "It was worth a shot." He set Copper's hoof down and put his hands on his hips. "Well, there goes that plan. I guess you can ride in the paddock while I look for this shoe."

"I guess." I looked around, and my eye fell on Misty, who was grazing with his back to us. "Or you could ride Misty."

"Really?"

"Why not? Hayley's gone back to bed and Mum's not home. Besides, someone has to and it's not going to be me."

"Give yourself a bit of time," he said reassuringly, looking at the grey pony with bright eyes. "I'm keen, if you reckon it'd be okay."

"Knock yourself out," I told him. "I can't imagine why you'd actually want to, but he's all yours."

"You're not enough of an adrenalin junkie," Jonty told me as he unbuckled Copper's halter and started towards Misty instead.

"I like my neck in one piece," I called to him, and he laughed.

Misty raised his head as Jonty approached, a wary look in his eye, then lifted his tail into the air and trotted to the other end of the paddock. I grinned.

"You're going to need a bribe."

Twenty minutes later, I was standing in the middle of our yard, staring at Rory's saddle and willing myself to get up there. The nerves were paralysing, and it was starting to frustrate me. *Stop being stupid,*

I told myself. *You've ridden Rory hundreds of times, and she's never once done anything bad. She's safe as houses.*

"You'll be right once you're on," Jonty said confidently. "Want a leg-up?"

"I'm good." I reached for the stirrup iron and caught it in my hand, then slipped my foot in. Took a deep breath, grabbed the pommel of the saddle, bounced on my toe once, then swung up into the saddle. It wasn't very graceful, and took more willpower than usual, but Rory stood like a statue as I scrambled onto her back. I found my offside stirrup, then reached forward to pat her sturdy bay neck.

"Good girl."

As usual, Jonty had been right. Now that I was on board, I didn't feel so nervous. And the reassuring, familiar sight of Rory's long neck and floppy ears ahead of me was a welcome change from Misty's solid, hard crest. I glanced over at the grey pony, who was spinning in circles around Jonty every time he lifted his foot to the stirrup.

"Stand still, you little bugger."

"He doesn't like you."

We both turned to see Hayley walking towards us with a bag of carrots in one hand. Jonty lowered his foot from the stirrup and looked at me guiltily.

"Copper threw a shoe," I explained. "So I asked him to exercise Misty instead."

Hayley shrugged, unfazed. "Fair enough."

She pulled a carrot out of the bag as she approached Misty, who nickered eagerly, his eyes shining in delight. Carrots were his favourite thing in the world.

"You don't mind?" Jonty asked her.

"Why would I?" Hayley broke a carrot in half and fed it to Misty, as Rory eyed up the carrots with interest, although she was too polite to move her feet until I told her to. "Here you go then, Rory Snorey," Hayley said, holding a carrot out towards my mare.

Outraged by the very suggestion of sharing his bounty, Misty lunged towards Rory with his ears pinned and teeth bared. Rory jumped back in alarm, her desire for a carrot completely overruled by an unwillingness to have her face bitten off. I took a breath and tried to calm my racing heart as Misty returned his attention to Hayley, pricking up his ears and looking as cute as possible to entice her to feed him more carrots. Hayley laughed, and gave him two.

Once he was done eating, Jonty lifted his foot to the stirrup again, but Misty spun away from him once more, crashing into Hayley and knocking her off balance. Jonty was quick to notice, grabbing my sister around the waist to stop her from falling.

"You okay?"

"I'm fine." She pushed him off, and tucked her hair behind her ears as she glared at Misty. "You little brat. How dare you?" Taking the reins from Jonty, she marched up to him, gathered the reins at the base of his neck, and lifted her foot up to the stirrup. "Now *stand*."

"Hayley –" I started to object, but she completely ignored me as she swung herself up onto Misty's back. She swayed slightly as she landed in the saddle, and I watched with my heart in my mouth as Misty stood stock still, all of his muscles tense.

Hayley picked up her other stirrup, shortened her reins, and clicked her tongue. Misty swung forward into his quick-striding walk, and my remonstrations died on my lips at the expression on my sister's face, looking happier than I'd seen her in months.

I nudged Rory up alongside Misty, removing my helmet and holding it out to Hayley. "At least put this on," I begged her.

She turned her head and grinned at me, a mischievous sparkle in her eye. "Come on Miss Safety First. Where's your sense of adventure?"

I watched helplessly as Hayley trotted Misty past me, through the open gate and into the jumping paddock. Her balance was still slightly off, her rising trot not as smooth and effortless as usual, but to his credit, Misty didn't take advantage. He seemed to be aware that he had to take care of his rider, and he trotted steadily along the fence line. In the far corner, Hayley nudged him into a canter, and Misty leapt forward eagerly. I could hear her laughing as she rode back towards us, her smile widening with every stride.

I was reminded, then, of the day that Misty had first arrived on our farm. He'd been a surprise Christmas present when Hayley was twelve, her first proper show jumping pony. She'd coveted him for years, always watching him at the shows, delighting in his exuberant leaps and bucks. She'd been convinced from the moment she first saw him that they were made for each other, had been certain she would be able to ride him better than anyone else, and when he'd come onto the market, she had demanded that Mum buy him for her. He hadn't been cheap, but she'd talked our parents into it, and he'd arrived here on Christmas Day. Hayley had taken him off the truck, jumped on him bareback, and cantered off around the paddock in a halter. We'd all watched with our hearts in our mouths, but Misty had behaved perfectly – until one of the chickens had appeared out of nowhere and startled him into a series of rodeo bucks. I'd been struck with terror just watching it happen, but Hayley had gripped on tight, still laughing as she gradually convinced Misty to stop bucking and come to a halt. Then she'd flung her arms around his neck, hugged him tight, and declared that he was the most perfect pony she'd ever met. I'd thought she was utterly mad and incredibly brave.

Some things never changed.

"Uh, Tess?"

I glanced at Jonty, then followed his line of sight to my father, hurrying down from the yards with his eyes fixed on Hayley.

"Oh crap."

I nudged Rory to turn her around, and rode in Dad's direction.

"I told her not to," I said quickly. "But you know how much she listens to me."

Dad watched Hayley as she cantered Misty in a circle, oblivious to his presence. His expression was inscrutable, but he didn't tell her to stop. He just watched her ride, listening to her laughter, which died quickly when she saw him. Sitting tall and resolute in the saddle, Hayley brought Misty back to a bouncy trot and directed him over to us.

"Let's hear it then," she told Dad defiantly as she halted in front of him. "Tell me I shouldn't have done that."

But Dad just shook his head as Hayley leaned forward and wrapped her arms around Misty's solid neck.

"You're the best pony in the whole world," she told him. "I don't know why Tess doesn't like you, but I will always love you the mostest of all."

Misty bobbed his head up and down, as if he was nodding agreement. Without further argument, Hayley slid her feet out of the stirrups and swung her leg over the saddle, landing shakily on the ground next to Misty, her hands clenching the saddle tightly to keep her balance. Dad put an arm around her shoulders and guided her away as Jonty took charge of Misty again, and we watched silently as Dad helped Hayley back to the house.

"How was your ride this morning?"

I sat down on the couch next to my father, who had his legs stretched out in front of him. There was a rugby game on TV and he was holding an open bottle of beer, but he didn't seem to be paying much attention to either of them. It was dinner time, but Mum and Hayley were still in Palmerston North, and we wouldn't eat until they returned.

"Fine."

"Rory behave herself?"

"Always." I picked at the chipped green polish on my toenails. "If I don't ride Misty, will you sell him?"

Dad looked surprised, then thoughtful. "I don't know. Would there be any point in keeping him?"

"Probably not."

"Well then, you probably have your answer."

"Hayley will kill me," I muttered.

The TV commentators started yelling excitedly as one of the yellow-jerseyed players started running full tilt down the rugby field. Dad and I watched as he dodged a tackler and threw himself over the try line, winning the game at the last minute.

Neither of us spoke.

7

FIASCO

I was up early on Saturday morning. It was the day of Hayley's party, and Mum was running around like a crazy person trying to get everything organised. I found her in the kitchen, pouring herself a second cup of strong coffee and barking orders down the phone to someone. I grabbed a glass of orange juice, then went out onto the porch and sat in the hammock, looking out across the rolling farmscape. It was a beautiful day, without a cloud in the bright blue sky. Colin licked my hand as I sipped the cold drink, watching the world wake.

The front door creaked as Mum pushed it open, and I turned to look at her.

"I'm going to need your help today."

"I know. AJ and Katy are coming at lunchtime to help me decorate the woolshed," I reminded her.

Hayley had insisted that Jonty couldn't be the only friend I invited to her party, as apparently it would make me look like a loser, which would reflect poorly on her. Katy and AJ were the only socially acceptable options I had, at least in Hayley's eyes, although their invitation came at the exclusion of Susannah, who Hayley couldn't stand. I was sick of following along with Hayley's politics, but her long-running feud with Susannah wasn't something I wanted to deal with in front of all the people who would be at the woolshed tonight, so I'd let it go.

"What about this morning, before they get here?" Mum asked as Dad appeared in the doorway behind her. "I don't want you sitting around doing nothing while I'm busting a gut trying to get everything done."

When do I ever sit around doing nothing? I wanted to ask her, but the look on my father's face made me back off.

"I've got to feed the horses, and muck them out," I told Mum, trying to maintain my composure. "And the farrier's meant to be coming to put Copper's shoe back on."

"No he's not, I put him off for a few days," she said dismissively. "There's no rush to get that horse shod, it's not like anyone's been riding him."

I wanted to ask if Jonty was invisible, but I held my tongue. She was irritable enough without me bringing him into it.

"I've got a few jobs that Tess can help with," Dad said, stepping out of the house and sliding his feet into his gumboots. Mum started to argue with him, but he stopped her. "If you want the boys to have time to clean up the yards around the woolshed, they need to get all their usual jobs done by lunchtime. Tess can help with those so they're free this arvo."

Even Mum couldn't argue with that logic, and I didn't want to give her the chance. I jumped up, draining the last of my orange juice before wiping my mouth with the back of my hand.

"I'm in. Where do you need me?"

"At least have some breakfast first," Mum grumbled, going back inside the house.

I rolled my eyes at Dad as I moved to follow her, but he put a hand on my shoulder and stopped me.

"Be kind," he said. "She's having a hard time right now."

"Aren't we all?" I asked him, noticing the dark shadows under his eyes.

He didn't confirm or deny it. "Just be patient with her, okay?" I nodded, and Dad squeezed my shoulder approvingly. "Atta girl."

I ate my toast as I walked up to the barn, enjoying the warmth of the sun on my bare arms. Misty was waiting at the gate, demanding that he get his breakfast, and he whinnied impatiently when he saw me. I gave him the last mouthful of my toast, which he snatched from my hand and scoffed down while aiming threatening kicks at Rory as she walked tentatively up behind him. I threw out a few biscuits of hay to them and Myrtle, who was sharing their paddock, then brought Copper up to the barn for his morning feed. He munched his way dreamily through it while I mucked out the paddock, which took twice as long as usual because I'd neglected to do it halfway through the week. By the time I was finished, Rory and Misty had polished off most of their hay, and Copper had almost finished his feed. I gave him some hay and left him to fill his belly while I went looking for my father.

Instead I found Bayard, who was on his way to clean the working dogs' kennels. It wasn't anyone's favourite job, but it went infinitely faster when two people did it, so I offered to assist him.

"Really?" he asked suspiciously.

"Yes, really. Dad said I should help you out, so here I am. Unless you know where my father is so I can ask him for something else to do."

"No, it's cool," he shrugged. "You can help."

"Gee, thanks."

Bayard smiled tentatively as I fell into step with him, and we walked in silence up to the kennels. The dogs were predictably pleased to see us, and we let them out to run around while we hosed out the kennels and shook out the mats of course sacking that they slept on. They were well-fed and given adequate shelter, but they weren't pampered. Dad subscribed to the theory that if dogs were too comfortable in their runs they wouldn't want to come out and work. I wasn't sure I agreed with him, but it wasn't my call to make. I was just grateful that Colin had been allowed to stay on the farm as my pet after he'd been sacked as a working dog for his lack of ability to focus.

Bayard and I had always worked well together, and we got the kennels done in record time. He'd never been much of a conversationalist, and despite recent events, it was easy to fall back into friendly habits. With our work done, we took the dogs for a short run up the hill, directing them into little thickets and behind rocky outcrops to try and start a few rabbits. Midge and Dusty caught one each, much to their immense pride, and Thor managed to start one, but was so shocked by its sudden appearance that he let it run between his legs and dive down a nearby hole before he even realised what was happening.

It wasn't until later, when the dogs were locked back up and we had moved into the workshop, trying to find the right equipment to repair a broken trough in the cattle yards, that Bayard decided to ruin things again. It started innocuously enough.

"Looking forward to the party tonight?"

"Yeah, sort of," I told him. "About as much as I look forward to anything that revolves entirely around Hayley."

He chuckled. "Isn't that the entire universe?"

"So she'd like to think," I muttered, then shook my head. "Am I a horrible person? I should be grateful that she's okay. Or I should be beside myself with worry that this operation might not work, like Mum is. I swear she's on the constant verge of a panic attack."

"Can't blame her for that," Bayard muttered, pulling a box of screws off the shelf and rummaging through it.

"I don't blame anyone for that. It's nobody's fault. Not even Hayley's. She didn't ask to get sick. But sometimes I feel like they're all taking it out on me."

"I'm sure they don't mean to."

"They don't. I know they don't. Jonty keeps telling me the same thing," I said. "But it's just hard…what?"

Bayard's expression had changed the moment I mentioned Jonty's name, but he shook his head.

"Spit it out, Bayard," I insisted.

His frown intensified. "I just don't get what you see in him."

"Well fortunately for you, that's none of your business, so you don't need to worry about it."

He just gave me a sceptical look. "I care about you, Tess."

"Good. So does he."

Bayard rolled my eyes. "That's what you think," he muttered.

I grabbed the box of screws and pulled it away from him.

"Stop it," I told him firmly. "Why do you keep acting like Jonty's the worst person in the world? What's he ever done to you?"

"It's not me that I'm worried about," Bayard said plaintively. "It's *you.*"

"Well you can stop. I think I know what's good for me and what isn't – and Jonty? He's good for me. You need to accept that."

He shook his head defiantly, meeting my eyes. "You think you know him, but you don't," he said. "You don't know what he's really like."

I couldn't believe what I was hearing. "And you do?"

Bayard reached for the box of screws, but I pulled them further away from him.

"I'm trying to work," he complained.

"And I'm trying to get you to explain yourself, so when I get what I want, you'll get what you want."

"You sound like Hayley."

"Good. She's a master at getting her own way. So let's hear it. What exactly don't I know about Jonty?"

Bayard clenched his jaw and looked straight at me, his blue eyes stony. "That you're far too good for him. That he's a drunk, just like his old man, and he's only going to drag you down."

My mouth literally fell open at the absurdity of that statement. Bayard reached over and grabbed the box of screws from me before I had time to react, then resumed his rummaging.

I found my voice at last. "Really?" I asked incredulously. "All this time and that's the best lie you can come up with?"

"It's true."

"It is not, and you know it." I ignored the first part and focused on the second. "I've known him for years and I've never once seen him drunk."

"I have." Bayard pulled a medium-sized screw out of the box and scrutinised it closely. "Heaps of times."

"When?" I demanded.

"Most recently, that day he missed school and told you he was at home sick. He wasn't."

I remembered that day last year. That's when Bayard's animosity had started. "How would you know?"

"Because I saw him," Bayard said certainly. "He lied to you about that, and God knows what else, and you just keep believing him. You're going to get hurt, Tess, and I don't want to see that happen."

My head was spinning, trying to process this information. None of it fitted in with the Jonty that I knew, that I'd known for years, and I couldn't work out why Bayard was saying it.

"Why should I believe you?"

"Why shouldn't you? I've never lied to you. Unlike him. And it wasn't just that one time, either. He's been sent home from school in the past for being drunk in class."

I didn't believe him. I couldn't. Not Jonty. He'd never been anything other than good to me, never anything other than stone cold sober. I just couldn't picture it, couldn't imagine it at all. Bayard had to be lying, but what I didn't understand yet was why.

"I've had enough of this," I snapped. "I don't know where it's all coming from, or why, but you need to stop. Jonty and I are dating, whether you, or my mother, or anyone else likes it or not! And if you can't handle that, then we can't be friends."

"So that's it?" Bayard asked angrily, throwing the screw onto the bench. It bounced onto the floor and rolled under a pile of wood. "You spend years telling me all the things that I do that you don't like, expecting me to change, but as soon as I say *one* thing to you that you don't want to hear, you cut me out of your life."

"It's not a little thing, Bayard!" I cried. "It's a ridiculous, false allegation against someone that I care about! And if that makes you jealous, too bad."

"I'm not jealous," he argued, but I noticed the way his skin flushed when he said that. "I'm saying this because it's *true*, Tess. Go ahead and ask him."

I shook my head. I wouldn't insult Jonty with even the suggestion. "Why don't you ask yourself, instead, why you're so insecure that you have to make up these ridiculous lies to try and ruin my life?"

Bayard shook his head. "You're the one who's going to ruin your life if you get involved with him."

"I'm *already* involved with him," I reminded Bayard. "And I'm happier than I've been in years, *because* of him. So you can take your lies and piss right off."

I marched to the door and pulled it open, letting sunlight flow into the dingy workshed.

"You're too good for him," Bayard said again, and I stared at his stupid back as he turned away, wishing I could punch him hard enough to make it hurt.

"I can't believe we used to be friends," I snapped, slamming the door shut behind me.

I walked back down to the house, where I was immediately pounced upon by my stressed-out mother, who started throwing chores at me like it was an Olympic sport. Fortunately, once Katy and AJ turned up a couple of hours later, I was able to escape with them to the woolshed, and we spent the afternoon stringing up fairy lights, making streamers, sweeping the old pine floorboards and setting out trestle tables for food. We laughed and chatted and pretended that everything was fine, and I pushed everything Bayard had said to the back of my mind, refusing to dwell on it.

When he turned up later with Jock to clean out the yards, I completely ignored them both, which wasn't entirely fair on Jock, but I was too angry to even look in Bayard's direction. It wasn't until they were finished and had left again that I went to inspect their work.

They'd done well, scraping the worst of the surface muck out of the sheep pens and spreading a thick layer of wood shavings on top, although nothing could disguise the pungent smell of sheep manure that lingered in the air.

"I'm not going to be able to eat anything in this stench," Katy declared, wrinkling up her nose.

"Because you're normally such a pig," AJ replied sarcastically. "Besides, I've seen you eat a bag of chips with horse shit all over your hands after mucking out, so you're just being a hypocrite."

"Horse shit is different. It doesn't smell as bad as this."

They both looked at me, and I shrugged. "Is it really that bad? I guess I'm just used to it."

Katy pulled a face, but AJ laughed. "Spoken like a true farmer."

The party was a resounding success, at least from Hayley's point of view. She revelled in the attention being showered upon her, sitting on a throne of hay bales in the corner of the woolshed, surrounded by people delivering gifts and glad tidings. I leaned against the wall opposite her, sipping a bottle of ginger beer and watching her, wondering if everyone could see the bags under her eyes, or noticed how much weight she'd lost. If they did, they didn't mention it. But then why would they? We were gathered there that night to celebrate the end of Hayley's radiation treatment. Over half of the people there didn't even know she was going to have surgery next week, and at least a third hadn't even known she was sick until they'd been invited to her recovery party. We were all there to smile and laugh and pretend that everything was fine. Only a handful of people knew the truth, and none of us were talking.

"Sorry I'm late."

I turned to look at Jonty as he stepped up next to me. He was wearing faded jeans, cracked boots with broken laces and a crumpled grey shirt that was two sizes too big, with the sleeves rolled up to his elbows. I caught sight of Bayard across the room, watching us. He was standing in a group of other local farming lads, all dressed in identical outfits – tan moleskins, woollen jerseys with zip collars, blue and white checked shirts, steel-capped boots. They all shopped at the same places, all wore the same brands – RM Williams, Back Country, John Bull – like an unofficial uniform. Jonty stood out like a sore thumb, and Bayard's voice came into my head again. *You're far too good for him.*

Shut up, Bayard.

"Hi. I was wondering where you were," I said. "Thought maybe you'd forgotten."

Jonty looked startled. "You think I could forget Hayley's special night?" he asked, turning towards my sister and giving her a brief wave.

I looked over in time to catch her waving back to him before turning her hand around and flipping him off.

Jonty shook his head at her. "And I thought *my* sisters were charming."

"Yours are," I told him, and he pulled a face.

"Only because they like you. That reminds me though, Morgan says that she likes that new book but not quite as much as *The Outsiders*, and Phoebe wants to know when you're actually going to come and have dinner with us." He raised an eyebrow speculatively, and I deflected the question.

"No message from Bella?"

"Not directly, but she tells me on a daily basis that you're the nicest person she knows."

I blushed. "Really?"

"Well, to be fair, she doesn't know that many people."

I punched him lightly on the arm, and he laughed and put his arm around my shoulders, squeezing me in towards him. I saw Bayard glance in our direction, and I stuck my tongue out at him before he turned away, a gesture that wasn't lost on Jonty.

"I take it you two haven't patched things up yet," he said idly, looking at Bayard's back which was pointed solidly towards us now.

"For a few minutes I actually thought we had," I admitted. "I ended up helping him clean the dog kennels this morning, which went fine, but then right afterwards he went back to bitching and moaning about you, so I walked out and..."

Jonty interrupted me with a frown. "About me? What about me?"

"Just the usual crap," I told him. "Don't worry. I told him to go to hell and ended up mopping the kitchen floor anyway. So all in all it was a stellar morning."

Jonty turned to look at Bayard, his expression slightly incredulous. "What's *the usual crap*?"

"It doesn't matter."

"Matters to me."

"It shouldn't. Honest, Jonty. Just ignore him."

Jonty shook his head. "Maybe I should ask him myself."

"Don't." I grabbed at the sleeve of his oversized shirt. I didn't want him to get into anything with Bayard, not with all of these people around. "Just let it go, okay?"

"I've *been* letting it go," Jonty told me, looking angry. "That's why it's still happening, and I've had a gutsful of it."

"But not now," I insisted, gripping his shirt sleeve harder. "Not tonight. Okay?"

He looked at me, his lips thinning into a tight line, then slowly nodded. But the moment I released his arm, Jonty started moving in Bayard's direction. "Where are you going?"

"To say hi to the boys," Jonty replied, catching Jock's eye. The young farmhand nodded a greeting to Jonty and waved him over. "I'll be right back."

Before I could say anything, I heard my name.

"Tess! C'mere for a sec!"

I ignored Hayley's summons, watching Jonty walk over to the group of boys who all turned to greet him. All except Bayard, who'd seen him coming and quickly veered off towards the food table, with one of the other guys flanking him.

"Tess!" I turned back to my sister who was gesturing irritably at me. "Come sit. We've had a brainwave."

I made my way towards her as Jonty was welcomed by Jock and his friends, who were all much friendlier than Bayard. With no choice but to leave him to it, I took a seat on a nearby hay bale and looked at my sister.

"What?"

"Katy's going to ride Misty in Pony of the Year."

I blinked at Hayley, then turned to look at Katy. "Really?"

"If you don't mind," Katy said quickly, but Hayley scoffed.

"Mind? She's thrilled, look at her. She's not going to ride him, so someone might as well. And at least I know you'll give him a good ride and finally do him justice."

Ouch. I smiled weakly at Katy, who was still looking a little anxious. "Sounds like a plan."

She broke into a wide smile. "Yeah? Awesome! I'm so excited! I've only got Molly in it this year and she's either perfect or a nightmare, depending on how she feels on the day. But Misty's the bomb."

"He'll always jump clean, he's super careful," Hayley said, warming to her favourite subject. "He can be spooky though, especially with the crowds. You'll have to jump him in the Stakes class the day before, to get him used to the Premier arena. He's been in there a bunch of times, but it's different every year, and he's been given a bit of a soft ride lately. Don't be afraid to be firm with him," she continued, oblivious to my feelings.

Katy nodded along, her attention fixed on Hayley, while AJ chatted to a couple of the local boys that were lingering around my sister, vying for her attention. Surrounded by people, I felt suddenly alone. I looked across the room again for Jonty, but he was gone.

"Hey Tess?"

I turned to see AJ looking at me and smiled, relieved to be no longer invisible. I could always count on AJ to make me feel like I mattered.

"Where's your bathroom?"

Well, at least it gave me something to do. I walked with AJ down to the house and showed her where to go, then waited for her on the porch. It was dark at last, the strings of woolshed lights sparkling in the distance. It was a beautiful night with a full moon, and more stars than I could hope to count. I sat on the front step and leaned back on my hands, gazing up at them and trying to feel infinite.

"That is *much* better," AJ declared as she came out of the house, wiping her damp hands on her jeans. "Thanks."

I stood up reluctantly, rubbing the crick in my neck, and we walked back up the track towards the woolshed.

"You're so lucky, you know. Getting to live here."

"I know."

The tall macrocarpa trees rustled in the slight breeze, and the moonlight glinted off the dog runs as we passed them. Ruru hooted in the treetops, audible over the crunching of our feet across the dry grass, and I tried to imagine living somewhere else, but it wasn't something I could even properly comprehend. Even going away to study at university was going to be a struggle. Could I live without the open air, the barking of the dogs, the smell of lanolin on my hands, the rhythm of a steady horse beneath me? Could I walk on concrete footpaths instead of muddy farm tracks? Not for long, and certainly not forever.

Back at the woolshed, AJ veered off towards the drinks table.

"I'm gonna get another drink. You want something?"

"I'm good," I told her. "I'm gonna go find Jonty."

AJ fluttered her eyelashes at me and pretended to swoon. "Well then, I'll leave you to it. Have fun!"

We split up, AJ heading towards the bar while I wandered back inside. Jonty wasn't there, so I went back out and looked around the sheep pens. But I still couldn't find him. There was plenty of alcohol at the party tonight, and nobody was really supervising its consumption, so if Jonty was going to get drunk, here was his opportunity.

"Tess!"

A sharp whistle pierced through the air and I turned to see Hugh, standing with a couple of other men in one corner of the sheep yards.

I walked over to him. "Did you just whistle at me?"

"Sorry," he said, having the grace to look a little sheepish. "Force of habit. Where's Jonty?"

I shrugged. "Your guess is as good as mine."

Hugh frowned, then nodded over towards the gate with an ominous expression. I turned to see Nate Fisher standing in a small group of men, knocking back a rum and coke.

"Was he invited?" Hugh asked suspiciously.

"Not as far as I know." I watched Nate smack his lips as he finished his drink and headed towards the bar.

"Then I suggest that you find Jonty," Hugh said. "Tell him to get his old man home."

Something inside me bristled. "It's a party, Hugh," I pointed out. "I'm sure Nate's not the only one who just turned up without an invite. What's the big deal?"

Hugh put a hand on my arm and led me away from his companions, then lowered his voice. "You know as well as I do that Nate Fisher spends more time in the drunk tank on weekends than he does at home." He seemed surprised by my expression. "You don't know that? You should. I can't count the number of times I've seen him staggering out of there on a Sunday morning."

I knew that Hugh was an avid churchgoer, and would typically be in town on a Sunday to bear witness to that. Bayard's words came rushing back to me.

He's a drunk, just like his old man.

Not Jonty. He wasn't his father, was nothing like him. But it seemed like he was perpetually having to clean up after him.

"I'll find Jonty," I told Hugh, and walked away.

As it turned out, that was easier said than done. It took me at least fifteen minutes and several circuits of the sheep yards to discover that Jonty was nowhere in sight, and neither was Jock, or any of the friends he'd gone to talk to when I'd last seen him. I was on the verge of giving up when I caught a glimmer of light from the tractor shed on the other side of the paddock. Bereft of options, I went to investigate, stumbling a time or two on the uneven ground as I walked. I could hear their voices as I passed the hay barn, and I headed down the row of equipment bays to find six or seven boys sitting on the big flatbed trailer at the far end. As I approached, I heard the clink of glass bottles, and laughter as one rolled off the trailer and clinked onto the stones. I stumbled over yet another tuft of grass and grunted involuntarily. The voices ahead of me quietened, then one spoke out.

"Who's there?"

I regained my balance and stepped into the light, scanning their faces and looking for Jonty. He saw me before I found him, and immediately slid across the flat wooden deck of the trailer towards the edge.

"Hey Tess. What's up?"

"I've been looking everywhere for you."

I ignored the hoots of the other boys, scanning their faces and looking for Bayard, but he wasn't there. Jock was, and he gave me a friendly nod as he sculled back his bottle of beer.

Jonty jumped off the trailer and came over to me. "Found me."

"Did you know that your dad's here?"

I could tell immediately from his face that he didn't. A moment of shock, then resignation. "Where is he?" he asked, his shoulders slumping in defeat.

I pointed. "Over at the yards somewhere. Hugh's keeping tabs on him."

Jonty winced and started walking quickly back towards the woolshed. I hurried to keep up with him, but he was moving faster than I could in the dark.

"Wait up," I told him, but he didn't slow down as he looked over his shoulder at me.

"Thanks for the head's up. You should go hang out with your friends again."

"But you…"

As we passed the hay barn, the sound of a glass bottle hitting the concrete floor stopped me in my tracks.

"What was that?" I took a few steps towards the barn, squinting into the dark hollow of its entrance. "Hey! You're not allowed in there!" I called into the darkness.

"Leave it, Tess." Jonty's hand was on my arm, his voice soft.

"There's someone in there," I insisted. "What if they break glass in the hay, or spill beer on it and it goes mouldy?"

"We'll check it out in the morning, when we can see what we're doing," he said quickly. "Promise. But I've gotta go." He stepped in close to me and gave me a quick kiss on the forehead. "I'll see you tomorrow."

He turned and walked away from me again, and this time I let him go.

I recruited AJ and Katy to come back to the hay barn with me and make sure that no damage was being done. AJ was up for it, but Katy only joined us under extreme duress. I collected a heavy duty torch from the house and we walked back up to the barn, shining the bright beam across the grass in front of us as we went. But it was empty when we got there.

"Nothing but hay bales," AJ declared, making her way down the stacked hay in a series of jumps after checking the top row. "Maybe you were hearing things?"

"Jonty heard it too," I insisted.

"Well you obviously scared them off," Katy said as Jock and his friends came over to us.

"Are you playing Spotlight?" Jock asked.

"Not yet," AJ told him with a grin. "But that sounds like an excellent plan. Who's game?"

8

FAÇADE

I was up early the next morning and feeding the horses when I noticed someone climbing the bales in the hay barn. I threw another biscuit of hay to Copper and headed over there, knowing who I would find.

Jonty jumped down off the hay bales as I approached. "All clear. Whoever was in here last night left no trace."

"I know. I checked it out just after you left."

He nodded. "Fair enough. How'd the rest of the party go?"

"Fine. Broke up early in the end. Hayley got tired just before midnight and everyone dispersed pretty quickly after that. How's your dad?"

His face clouded over at the mention of his father. "Sleeping it off." He tilted his head to the side, looking at my face. "Is everything okay?"

I shook my head. I'd barely slept all night, my thoughts swirling madly around as I tried to forget all of Bayard's stupid comments. But as it had turned out, he hadn't been lying about Jonty's father, so now I needed to know the truth. The whole truth.

"We need to talk."

"Okay. What about?"

Where to start? I chewed my lower lip for a moment, then sat down on a hay bale and looked at him.

"What don't I know about you?"

Jonty blinked. "Lots of stuff, probably. D'you want a list?"

"I want to know why Bayard thinks…" I struggled to say the words out loud as Jonty looked at me anxiously.

"Thinks what?"

"That you're a drunk, like your old man." I made myself look at his face, and winced at his wounded expression. "I don't believe him. But I need to hear it from you."

Jonty sat down next to me. "I'm not a drunk. And I'm *nothing* like my old man."

I nodded, relieved. "I know." I clasped my hands together, staring at him. "What I don't know is why Bayard keeps saying all this."

Jonty took a deep breath, then let it out again. "I do."

A swallow flew into the hay barn and swooped up to its mud nest above the door, greeted by the twittering of its offspring.

"You remember last year, when I missed a day at school and he kept telling you to ask me why?"

I nodded. I'd refused at first, and when I had eventually broached the subject with Jonty, he wouldn't give me an answer. Instead he'd galloped off on Copper, and Misty had taken off on me in hot pursuit. Jonty's decision to jump the gate into the next paddock had led to me getting bucked off and having the wind knocked out of me. He'd been very apologetic, and I'd told him off for his recklessness, but I hadn't been given an answer. I'd never brought it up again.

"You said you were sick," I reminded him. "Bayard says you were lying."

"I didn't lie to you, Tess." Jonty turned his head and looked at me, sadness filling his light brown eyes. "I swear. My whole family had some bad fish the night before, and we were all laid up with it the next morning. My sisters didn't go to school either."

God, I wanted to believe him. "Then what's Bayard on about?"

Jonty ran his fingers through his hair. "He saw me in town that morning, and he got the wrong idea."

That made no sense. "Why were you in town if you were so sick?"

"I wasn't there by choice," Jonty said quietly. "I had to go get my dad."

He leaned forward, his elbows on his knees, and stared at the ground for a moment. Dust motes floated in the air around us, tickling my nose.

"We got the call from the cops to come fish him out of the drunk tank, and I was the only one who could get out of bed long enough to go do it. So I did." He cracked his knuckles, making me wince. "Sorry. Bad habit. I walked as far as the main road, then hitched a ride into town. I was feeling a bit better by then, but he was still sloshed. Cops just wanted him out of there. Hadn't even waited for him to sober up much. I dragged him out onto the street and he spewed all over the footpath." I watched Jonty's neck reddening as he spoke. "The smell, the sight of it… I made it to the gutter, at least, before I lost the last of that fish dinner." He wiped his mouth with the back of his hand reflexively as he relived the memory. "That's when Bayard and Hugh turned up. They were in town, picking up some fencing supplies. Hugh helped me get Dad onto the back of the ute, and gave us a ride home."

The pieces of the puzzle finally slotted together. "They thought you were drunk too," I realised.

Jonty shrugged, turning his head at last to look at me. "Yeah. Well, probably looked that way. I squared it up with Hugh later, explained the situation. I thought he believed me. Said he'd keep the whole thing quiet, and wouldn't say anything to your old man. As far as I know, he's kept his word. Bayard has too, but he's not happy about it."

"Why didn't you just tell me?"

"I didn't want you to know." He started to crack his knuckles again, then stopped. "I wanted you to like me."

I bit my lip, torn between the desire to give him a reassuring hug and the need to get more answers while he was in a sharing mood. I knew I'd regret it later if I didn't ask, so I went for it.

"That was once, but Bayard said he's seen you drunk lots of times." Jonty winced and looked away again, and I knew with certainty that once again, Bayard hadn't been lying. "Is that true?"

"Yeah."

I closed my eyes for a moment, then opened them again. "Can you tell me about it?"

"It was a few years ago." The muscles in his jaw clenched tighter, and he stared at the ground. "I'm not proud of it."

My thoughts shuffled around, trying to make sense of this new information, but it didn't fit. "Jonty, a few years ago you would've been like, twelve years old."

"I was eleven."

My world was rearranging itself inside my head. I searched for words, but only one would come to me. "Why?"

He glanced at me, looking like a puppy that had just been kicked. "It was the only way I could get through a day at school." He nudged a stone with the toe of his boot. The leather was cracked and split, the rubber sole coming away. "I've never been any good at sitting still, really. I was pretty hyper as a kid, always getting into trouble, always running around. Mum used to just send me outside to run around. Literally, she'd make me run laps around the house until I could sit still when I came inside." A trace of a smile flickered around his mouth. "School wasn't too bad at first, because they let little kids run around and play a whole lot, but the older I got, the harder it was to sit behind a desk all day. I got jittery, like there were ants crawling under my skin and I couldn't get them to stop. The teachers didn't get it. They thought I was naughty, or hyperactive. They eventually talked Mum into taking me to the doctor, and he gave me this medication that turned me into a zombie. I hated it. I couldn't think clearly, and I started struggling with schoolwork that had been easy for me before that. Mum was worried, but I wasn't getting in trouble at school anymore, so everyone just let it be."

The swallow swooped out of the building again, back into the sunlight. Jonty ran both of his hand backwards and forwards through his hair, making it stick up in all directions, then clasped his hands in front of him again, elbows still resting on his knees.

"Then Dad lost his job, and we were struggling to make ends meet. He's not the kind of guy who puts anything away for a rainy day, you know? Money ran out as fast as he could drink it, and I told Mum that I didn't need the meds anymore, that I'd be fine without them. She was so stressed, trying to pay rent and put food on the table, so she agreed. But whatever was in those pills had messed me up. I came off them cold turkey, and I felt like I was losing my mind. I couldn't sit still for five minutes, let alone five hours. I drove my family insane, constantly chattering, constantly moving around. One night, Dad shoved a bottle of bourbon in my hand and told me to drink until I calmed down. And it worked, so I kept doing it. Of course, the whole thing backfired on him when I started nicking his booze. He gave me a proper hiding when he figured it out, but it didn't stop me."

"Your mum must've been thrilled."

Jonty turned his head slightly in my direction, but still wouldn't meet my eyes. "She didn't know, at first. Didn't know for ages, actually. I got pretty good at hiding it from her, and I only drank when I was away from home. It wasn't until I turned up to school properly wasted one day, and got sent home. Then she worked it out real quick."

"Was she furious?"

He nodded. "Yeah. Lit into me, told me she'd married a drunk but she sure as hell wasn't going to raise one. Then…then she just sat there and cried." His voice shook on the words, and I moved closer, and put my arm around him, leaning my head against his shoulder. I felt him take a deep breath, his body held tense against mine. "I can't believe I'm telling you this. I'm sorry."

"Don't be," I told him. "Unless you're still getting drunk at school every day and I just haven't noticed."

He let out a low chuckle. "No way. I haven't touched the stuff since. That all happened before we moved out here," he added. "Man, I was so excited to live on a farm. So much space, so much room to run, you know?"

I knew. Dad had let Jonty's family move into the falling-down cottage out of charity because it was almost Christmas and they had nowhere else to go. But Jonty had got on everyone's last nerve pretty quickly when he'd been found running all over the farm, and after he'd left a gate open and let stock out into the hay paddock, Dad had told him to stay off our land.

"I remember," I told him. "I also remember coming home from grocery shopping one morning and finding you in the paddock riding Misty without a saddle or bridle."

"Oh, man. Your dad scared the shit out of me that day." He rubbed his hair again, and a cowlick stuck up at the back. I reached up and gently smoothed it back into place.

"You could've been killed," I reminded him. "Of all the ponies to just get on and ride tackless, you went and picked Misty?"

"He was fine," Jonty insisted. "I was way too big for Tani by then, and he's never exactly been the most exciting pony to ride, especially after I got him to quit bucking me off every day. Misty was like a bullet train. I knew I shouldn't have been doing it, but I got addicted."

I pulled a face. "I can't empathise with that at all. Wait a second. Are you saying you did it more than once?"

His skin reddened. "Maybe."

"How many times?"

Jonty turned his head and looked at me bashfully. "I don't know. Six or seven?"

I sat back against the hay bales and stared up at the roof. "Are you insane?"

Jonty leaned back next to me with a crooked smile. "After everything I just told you, d'you really need to ask?" The smile didn't quite reach his eyes, and he swallowed hard as he looked at me, trying to gauge my mood.

I reached up and put one hand on his cheek, then drew him in towards me and kissed him. He sighed with relief and kissed me back. For a long moment that's all there was – just me and him, pressed against the hay bales in the morning sun.

"Wait a second," I said, pulling away from him. "I need you to promise me something."

"Anything."

"Promise you're not going to turn into a drunk."

Jonty met my eyes, and with the most serious expression I'd ever seen on his face, drew a cross over his heart. "I swear on my life. *Never.*"

"Okay." I leaned back in towards him, but he put a finger over my lips.

"Don't I get a promise from you?"

I sat up straighter. "What do you want?"

"Hmm." He looked at me consideringly. "So many things."

I slapped his arm playfully. "Pick one."

"I want you to start looking after yourself."

I blinked at him. "What's that supposed to mean?" I looked down at my stained polo shirt and faded shorts. "You want me to be more like Hayley, get all dolled up before I even leave the house?"

"No! God, no. Please don't do that," Jonty said quickly, genuine alarm in his voice. "That's not what I meant. I just want you to look out for yourself more. To stop doing things just because other people think you should. Or shouldn't," he added.

"Ah. So I should ignore my mother's advice to kick you to the kerb?" I joked.

Jonty blanched. "Did she say that?"

"No. Not exactly. Hey," I said, putting a hand on his cheek and making him look at me. "Don't worry about her. Because I'm going to make you that promise. I'm gonna go after what *I* want. And that will always include you."

We walked back towards the house, hand in hand. My stomach was rumbling furiously, but I ignored it. I felt like a weight had been lifted off my chest, and I suspected that Jonty felt the same way. At least until he spoke again.

"Does your mum really hate me?"

I squeezed his hand tighter. "No, of course not."

"But she doesn't like me being with you."

"There are a lot of things about me that my mother doesn't like," I told him. "You're just adding to the list." He looked worried, and I stopped walking. He stopped next to me, and I put my arms around his waist and looked at him. "She doesn't *hate* you. She doesn't even know you."

"Does that mean I should hang around more?"

"Hmm." I thought about that for a moment. It appealed to me, but I wasn't sure Mum would agree. "Just keep on making yourself useful."

He showed me a crooked smile. "I can do that," he agreed, leaning in and kissing me softly.

"Or you could just kiss her daughter right in front of the kitchen window," I murmured to him as we broke apart.

Jonty's face went white, and he spun around to look at the house in alarm. I laughed. "Relax, Casanova. She'll be sleeping off a hangover of her own this morning."

He glared at me, shaking his head. "I'm gonna get you for that one."

"Oh yeah?" I asked. "How, exactly?"

"I'm sure I'll come up with something." He kissed me again, then pulled back with a frown and sniffed my neck. "Did you shower this morning?"

"Yes."

There was a glint in his eye that I knew too well by now. "Are you sure?"

I took a step back, but he was too quick. Like lightning, his hand grabbed my wrist and pulled me in towards him, arms circling my waist tightly.

"Don't you dare," I warned him.

"Tess." He looked at me with the most innocent expression he could muster up, but I wasn't fooled. "Where's your faith in me?"

I had no time to respond, because moments later he'd picked me up and slung me over his shoulder. I kicked and screamed, thumping his back with my fists, but Jonty ignored my protestations, marching over to the big circular water trough in the middle of the paddock and dumping me unceremoniously into it.

I shrieked as I hit the murky green water, arms and legs flailing. He was laughing his head off as I scrambled out, soaked from head to toe.

"You are *so* gonna pay for that!"

I shook my head, dirty water spraying out in droplets around me, then spied the perfect weapon. The horses had been in this paddock a couple of days ago, and Copper was notorious for leaving sloppy manure behind him every time he went onto new pasture. Before Jonty realised what was happening, I'd scooped up a handful of shit and smushed it into his hair. He yelped and ran backwards, slipped on another poo and fell on his butt.

"What on earth are you two doing?"

Hayley was leaning on the gate to the paddock and staring at us both with great disdain. I looked down at myself, dripping with green trough water, then over at Jonty. A clump of manure slid down his cheek as he got to his feet, leaving a trail of muck behind it.

"Foreplay," Jonty told her as he put his arm around me, squeezing me tight against his chest. I leaned into the embrace, at least until he took advantage of my closeness and started rubbing his mucky hair against my face. I shrieked and pushed him off.

"You're disgusting. Both of you," Hayley told us from the gate, then turned to me. "Pancakes?"

I nodded, walking over to her. "Sure. I better have another shower first though."

Hayley wrinkled her nose. "Definitely. I don't want cow shit in my pancakes."

"It's horse shit," I told her.

"Because that's *so* much better."

"It's a little better," I replied. "It's only been through one stomach!"

9

FARM RIDE

The truck rolled into the farmyard at half past nine the next morning, arriving just as I was walking out to the horse paddock to catch the ponies. Katy jumped down from the cab almost before it had stopped moving and ran over to me, grinning with excitement.

"Hi Tess!"

She held out her hand for a halter, and I passed Misty's to her. She'd come to pick him up and take him home for the week and a half that remained before the Horse of the Year Show, but first we were going for a ride over the farm, while her mum drove their truck down to Opiki to pick up a pony that needed schooling. Misty and Katy would be collected on the way back, and then the little grey devil would be out of my life - for a couple of weeks, at least.

I turned around to wave goodbye to Katy's mum, but she had parked the truck by the barn, and a familiar face was lowering the hydraulic ramp. I looked at Katy in surprise, and she grinned back at me.

"Surprise! AJ came too. She wanted to bring Squib on a proper farm ride, now that she's *finally* allowed to ride again. It's okay, right?"

"Of course." I watched the ramp settle onto the gravel, and saw AJ bound up towards the pony that stood behind the divider. But it wasn't Squib. It was a dark bay with a glossy coat, and I recognised Forbes a moment before Susannah also appeared. She waved briefly to me before heading up the ramp to collect her pony from AJ.

I glanced at Katy, who offered me a hopeful expression. "AJ told Susannah the plan like an hour ago, and she said she wished she could come too, because she needs to get Forbes out and about more, and AJ invited her. By the time it occurred to AJ that you and Susannah aren't exactly the best of friends, her dad was already halfway to ours with Forbes in their truck, so it was kind of hard to say no."

She gave me a pleading look, and I did my best to smile reassuringly.

"It's fine," I told her. "I have no problem with Susannah, and Hayley's not here, so…"

My sentence trailed away as I thought about my sister. She'd gone off to hospital last night to be prepped for the surgery that was scheduled to happen today. It was one of the reasons that I'd agreed to Katy's farm ride idea, as a way to keep my mind off everything. Katy and I started walking towards the paddock to catch the ponies, and I handed her the carrots that she would need to bribe Misty.

We caught the ponies fairly easily, as Misty was excited by the presence of new ponies in our yard, and desperate to come closer. We'd tied them up in front of the barn and started grooming when AJ came over, greeting me with a warm hug.

"Thanks for letting us come!" she grinned. "I'm so excited to ride over your farm. Squib can't wait to get up some serious hills."

I smiled back at her, my stomach squirreling. I'd been riding regularly, and Rory was her usual dependable self, but I'd been sticking to short rides and easy tracks. My nerves weren't entirely back under control, so I'd planned to take Katy on a fairly gentle hack, trusting Misty to keep it exciting on his own. But AJ was clearly expecting an adventure, and I didn't want to let her down.

At least you're riding Rory, I reminded myself, patting my pony's neck reflexively. *Not much can go wrong with her.*

"Is Jonty coming with us?" AJ asked.

"No. Copper threw a shoe last week and we haven't had the farrier out yet. And anyway, he's busy."

AJ frowned, and put a hand on my arm. "Is everything okay with you two?"

"Yeah. Why?"

"You guys just seemed kinda distant, at the party."

I smiled at her. "That was...it was nothing. We're good. Solid. He's helping Hugh fix the fences on the back boundary today." My smile widened at the recollection of how thrilled Jonty had been to be asked.

"Where's Misty's tack?" Katy asked, and I took her into the tack room and showed her where to find it. Her mother came in too and I helped her carry out the trunk of Misty's blankets and boots and miscellaneous gear that I'd packed up for him last night.

"Thank you so much for this," Deb said as we shoved it into their truck's accommodation space.

"No, thank *you*," I told her. "Seriously."

Deb smiled and put an arm around my shoulders, giving them a quick squeeze. "She'll be okay," she said reassuringly. "She's a warrior, your sister."

I nodded, pretending to believe her. "Yeah, I know."

"Okay let's go!" AJ said, clipping up the chinstrap of her helmet and preparing to mount. "Come on slow pokes, we've gotta get moving!"

Five minutes later, we were all mounted and riding out of the yard. Rory started in the lead but was swiftly overtaken by Misty and Squib, who were quickly embroiled in a battle of who was going to be in front. Squib was marching forward with his head high and ears pricked, looking around him in interest as Misty jig-jogged next to him, tossing his head impatiently and demanding that we start cantering already. I watched him curiously, listening to Katy laughing at his antics. He was the same way for Hayley – always jogging, never wanting to walk – but he'd quit doing it with me, I supposed because I was always trying to keep him as calm as possible. That didn't seem to be Katy's priority.

Susannah's pony Forbes fell into place next to Rory, spooking at every leaf that moved and jumping sideways into my pony on regular occasions.

"Sorry," she apologised again as a pukeko ran out from underneath a flax bush, startling him.

"It's okay. He's pretty jumpy," I commented, wincing as her stirrup iron collided with my ankle bone for the third time in under a minute.

"Terrified of life," Susannah agreed. "He needs more outings like this. I've kept him a bit too sheltered since he came to me." I looked at her in surprise, unaccustomed to hearing her admit to her own shortcomings. "Thanks for letting us join you."

"Any time," I said reflexively, and Susannah shot me a genuine smile, although it disappeared quickly when a kereru flapped out of the trees ahead, its wings thrumming distinctively as it flew across our path. Forbes hit the brakes with force, almost unseating Susannah, then stood stock still and snorted in alarm at the sight of such a cumbersome bird in flight.

"Forbes, honestly, it's just a bird," Susannah muttered, nudging him with her heels.

"Come on Susannah, keep up," Katy called from up ahead, attempting to bring Misty to a halt as they waited for us to catch up. Misty couldn't keep still, shifting back and forward from one foot to the next, as if he was standing on hot coals. I'd never realised that Katy had such a hot seat. Misty had already broken out in a light sweat after only a few minutes of walking up the track.

We caught up and carried on past the sheep yards. There were stock in the pens, bleating furiously, and Squib slowed down to stare at them while Misty attempted to grab the bit and barge past him. Forbes sucked back until his head was level with my heel, letting

Rory take the lead and save him from potential sheep-induced doom, while my pony walked calmly on a loose rein, completely unfazed.

Dad came out of the yards and waved to me, and I drew Rory to a halt by his side.

"Looks like a party," he commented, scanning our group.

"Katy's here to pick up Misty," I explained. "And AJ and Susannah brought their ponies along for a ride."

Dad nodded. "Good idea. Where're you headed?"

I shrugged. "Nowhere special. We'll probably just go up Walker's Ridge, ride along to Table Top and then come back past the old farm."

"Huh." He looked at my friends, then back at me. "You got enough time to go a different way, do us a favour?"

AJ and Katy had ridden back to us, and they looked at each other as Misty pawed the ground impatiently.

"Hours," Katy said. "Mum's going down to Opiki to pick up a pony for schooling, but she's planning to visit friends while she's there. We've got all day, if we want it."

Dad nodded, scratching the back of his neck. "Well if you feel like doing some proper farm work, you could ride north and push the draft mob down the gully onto Stony Flat."

"Uh…"

Doubts assailed me as I wondered whether Rory was fit enough for that ride, whether my friends were going to be any kind of use when it came to shifting sheep, and whether their ponies would make it up the switchback without falling off the edge, because it took a steady, sure-footed horse to get up that narrow path. But Katy, AJ and Susannah were already expressing their willingness to help, so it appeared that our plans had officially changed.

"Take a couple of dogs with you to bark them up," Dad said. "Leave the gates onto the flat open, there's enough feed down there to hold them and we'll pick up the stragglers in a couple of days."

"Okay." I shifted in my saddle, rubbing Rory's neck and thanking providence yet again that I was riding her and not Misty for what now promised to be several hours in the saddle. "Anything else?"

"Just take a look at the yards down there for us," Dad said. "Give us a head's up on what kind of condition they're in and if they need any repairs done."

"Will do."

Dad clapped Rory on the neck, nodded to my friends, and went back to what he'd been doing. I nudged Rory into action, turning her around and riding back the way we'd just come.

Squib hurried up alongside me, and I turned towards AJ's smiling face.

"Back this way, is it?"

"No, it's that way," I said, pointing out towards the hills. "But if we're going all the way out to Stony Flat, we'll need to pack some lunch."

Half an hour later we headed out again, our saddlebags now bulging with sandwiches that had been hastily cobbled together in the kitchen by me and AJ while the other two sought – and gained – permission from their respective parents to be later than we'd planned. Water bottles had been clipped to saddles, and warm clothing was fastened across the front, because I knew from experience how cold it could get on top of the ridge, even on a sunny day like this.

"Colin, go back," I told my dog, who'd followed us from the house. He stopped and looked at me sadly, his ears and tail drooping.

"Aw, let him come," AJ said sympathetically. "Your dad said we needed to take dogs."

"We need farm dogs who can actually work stock," I said mercilessly. "Trust me, Colin's more trouble than he's worth when it comes to doing real work. Go on, go home," I repeated, and Colin slunk slowly back to the house.

"Callous," AJ teased me. "He'll never forgive you now."

"He'll have forgotten all about it by the time we get back, trust me," I said. "And unless you want it to take five hours longer than it should, with sheep scattered six ways to Sunday, we don't bring him along on musters."

"I'm not sure that Forbes is going to be much use either," Susannah said from behind me, and I looked over my shoulder at her. "He's more likely to run away from the sheep than herd them."

"He'll be okay," I told her. "He can stay at the back with Rory. She'll protect him."

We rounded the corner to where the kennels were located under the stand of macrocarpa trees that sheltered them from the worst of the weather. Several dogs were out working, but there were a few still in their runs. I kicked my feet out of the stirrups and swung to the ground as AJ rode up alongside me.

"Want me to hold her?" she offered, holding out her hand for Rory's reins.

"She's fine," I assured AJ. "She'll stand."

True to my word, Rory stood perfectly still as I left her, walking up to the kennels and looking at the dogs, each of them pleading to be chosen for whatever adventure lay ahead. I unlatched Cave's gate and he jumped down eagerly, wagging his tail and barking loudly.

"All right, all right, I chose you, calm down," I told him, giving his head a quick rub before scanning the rest of the crates.

"What about this one?" AJ called, and I turned to see where she was pointing.

"That's a heading dog."

"Um, it says on the gate that her name is Pink, not *That*," AJ said. "And why can't we take her?"

"Because we don't need her. We want the Huntaways to bark the sheep down, and the natural landscape will funnel them towards the gate once they start moving. Besides, Dad'll want Pink later on." I reached Thor's kennel, and he licked my hand through the grate.

"Come on then, you."

I opened the gate and Thor jumped down excitedly. Cave took one look at him and then fixed me with a withering expression, clearly not impressed by my choice of teammate.

"You can show him the ropes, Cave," I told the older dog. "Come on now."

I swung back up into Rory's saddle and whistled the dogs, who fell into step with us, tails high and ears pricked, keen for adventure.

We headed out across the farm, Cave trotting along beside Rory like a model citizen while Thor ranged ahead, flushing rabbits out of the bushes with his deep bellowing barks. Forbes leapt out of his skin every time Thor spoke, almost unseating Susannah more than once, and clung increasingly close to Rory who he had selected as his security blanket. Squib marched along at the front, his big stride leaving the rest of us behind so that AJ had to repeatedly stop and wait for us, and Misty continued to jig-jog just ahead of Rory, his light grey coat turning dark with sweat.

AJ reached a junction in the race and stopped, looking around.

"Where to?" she asked me over her shoulder.

I looked at the hills ahead of us, then pointed left. "That way. We'll take the longer way round, since we've got time, and it's a nicer ride up through the forestry."

"Uh, is it a pine forest?" Susannah asked dubiously, and I nodded.

"Don't tell us Forbes is scared of pine trees too," AJ said with a grin, while Katy snickered.

"Of course he's not, I took him up into the pines behind ours loads of times," Katy said, reminding me that Forbes had been her pony before he'd been Susannah's.

But Susannah had a different reason to hesitate. "I'm allergic to pine pollen."

"Oh." I halted Rory and looked around. "Well, there is another way. It's just…it's a bit more challenging."

AJ's face lit up. "I'm up for it. How about you guys?"

Katy shrugged. "Sure. Bring it on."

Only Susannah was hesitant. "Define *challenging*."

I pointed straight ahead of us. "See those hills?" They all nodded. "We're headed to the other side. And see that trail zig-zagging up the one on the left?"

They all stared for a moment, then Susannah spoke.

"I'm not *that* allergic. I'll just cover my face or something."

"Don't be such a wimp," AJ said. "Squib's keen, and so am I. Bring it on, I say!"

"You would," Katy laughed. "But Misty's been up before, right?" I nodded, and she grinned. "So I'm in."

Rory had been up it a few times as well, and even down it once, though that was an experience I never intended to replicate. I looked at Susannah, who was frowning at the steep, narrow trail.

"Come on Susannah, put your big girl undies on and give it a go," Katy teased.

"If Forbes gets hurt, my dad will *kill* me," she said worriedly.

"He's not going to get hurt. Tess, how many horses have actually fallen off that trail?"

"Four," I said, then grinned as AJ's face blanched. "I'm kidding. None, as far as I know, but our horses are all well used to the farm tracks and they know how to pace themselves."

"We'll be fine," AJ insisted. "Come on. Live a little!"

The hill was even steeper than I'd remembered, and the higher you climbed, the steeper the drop-off on the side became. Rory walked solidly along, blowing heavily with the unaccustomed exertion and taking careful, sure steps up the narrow track that the sheep had forged over the years. It was only just wide enough for us to go up in single file, and Forbes was behind me, his nose pressed against Rory's tail despite Susannah's attempts to get him to back off. Fortunately for him, she was well-mannered enough that she just put up with it.

Ahead of me, Misty was scrambling up the track, desperate to keep up with Squib's big-striding walk, which had barely slowed even as we headed up the steep hill. AJ was looking around with interest, laughing carelessly even as Squib dislodged a rock under one of his hooves and sent it skittering over the edge of the slope. I turned my head and watched it go, bouncing down the side of the hill into the gorse.

Behind me, Susannah had her eyes fixed firmly ahead, and she looked slightly green.

"You okay?"

She nodded without speaking, and I looked ahead to where Misty had just reached another switchback in the trail. He cut the corner, jumping up the bank instead of making a smooth turn, and Katy yelped, grabbing a chunk of his mane as he went.

We climbed up and up and up, pausing just over halfway to let the ponies catch their breath. Even Misty's sides were heaving, and he'd finally quit jig-jogging, which must have been a relief for Katy.

"This is amazing," AJ said, turning in her saddle and looking out at the view. You could see most of the farm from here, the rolling hills glowing gold in the sunlight. "I've said it before and I'm gonna say it again. You're *so* lucky to get to ride up here every day."

"Nobody in their right mind would ride up here every day," Susannah muttered from behind me, and I grinned at her.

"How much of that land is yours?" Katy asked me, and I pointed out our boundaries as Cave came scrambling along the side of the hill, panting heavily but still full of running. Thor was ranging ahead, full of youthful enthusiasm.

"Ready to keep going?" AJ asked as Squib started shuffling his feet restlessly. "Squib's had enough of the view."

"Yeah. Grab a fistful of mane once you're around the next corner," I warned her. "Part of the track broke away a few years ago so they have to kind of scramble up it. Just give them their heads and hold on."

Susannah looked concerned. "Should I get off and lead him?" she asked, sliding her feet out of her stirrups.

"No," I said quickly. "Not a good idea. You don't wanna give him the option to push you off the edge." She turned even greener at the thought. "You'll be fine. Just let him keep sticking to Rory like glue. He'll be a mountain goat by the time we're done." I nodded up to AJ. "Let's keep going. We'll stop for sandwiches at the top."

She clicked her tongue to Squib, who dug his toes in and we were off again.

The view from the top was almost worth the death-defying access to it. We halted the blowing ponies on top of the hill and dismounted, giving them a moment to recover while we ate our sandwiches. AJ insisted on sharing hers with Squib, which I thought was a waste of perfectly good human food.

"You're going to be starving later," I warned her as she fed half of her sandwich to her pony.

"He likes it," she said. "Just because you guys are heartless, unsharing types."

"They're ponies. They can eat grass," I reminded her. "And don't feed the dogs either." Katy shot me a guilty look as Thor sat at her feet, drooling up at her adoringly. "They're working dogs. They get fed once a day."

"Sorry," she told Thor, patting him on the head. "You have very strict parents."

I stood next to Rory, the smell of her sweat filling my nostrils. Thin rivulets of sweat were running down her face, and her sides were going in and out like bellows. Poor pony wasn't really fit enough for this ride, and I rubbed her neck apologetically. The farm stretched out below us, the road winding like a ribbon through the dry brown paddocks. I could see my house, the barn, the woolshed and stock yards. Up the road in one direction was the original farmhouse, where Hugh lived with two of the other farmhands, and down the road in the other direction was the ramshackle cottage where Jonty lived.

There was barely a cloud in the sky, and the breeze that reached us on top of the hill was mild. I stared at the bright blue expanse overhead, willing it to rain. If we didn't get rain soon, we were going to have to start destocking. I concentrated on that problem, running possible solutions through my head, trying to think of anything that wasn't worrying about Hayley. I'd managed to forget about her for the twenty minutes that it had taken us to climb the switchback, but she kept coming back into my head. I checked my watch for the time. Still half an hour before she went into surgery. And that was assuming it was running on time, which my limited experience of hospitals told me was unlikely.

"Can I just say that I totally get it now?"

I turned and looked at AJ, who was staring out towards the distant horizon. "Get what?"

"Why you don't care about show jumping." I felt my face redden slightly at her words, but she was being serious. "I mean it. I always assumed that people who didn't want to jump were either Nervous Nellies or just deeply boring types who enjoyed dressage," she explained, pulling a face. "People who go round and round in circles for fun. But this..." and she swept her arm wide, gesturing to the wide expanse that lay before us. "This is a blast. If I could do this every day, I'm not sure I'd be bothered with show jumping either."

"I would," Katy said. "No offence, Tess. This is nice, but it's not show jumping."

"I'm not sure that I don't qualify as a Nervous Nellie," I told her. "Since all I do when I *do* go jumping is hold on tight, close my eyes and pray that I'll make it to the other side."

"No you don't," Katy contradicted me. "You've been riding awesome this season. That lesson at Susannah's was just a bad day. Don't let it ruin everything else that you achieved."

"Are you going to stay on the farm after you finish school?" AJ asked as we remounted and rode on down the sloping ridgeline.

"I don't know," I admitted. "I want to. I guess it depends."

"On what?"

I shrugged. "A few things." I looked around us. "If this drought doesn't break soon, we might not have a farm much longer."

AJ winced. "Is it that bad?"

"No. I'm being dramatic." Rory scrambled carefully down a low bank. Squib leapt off it, landing several feet away and adding a buck for dramatic effect. Katy shouted something and we looked back to see Misty cantering sideways, foaming at the mouth as he attempted to follow, while Forbes teetered on the edge, peering down nervously at the solid ground only a foot below.

"Bunch of nutters," AJ said, watching them affectionately. "Bet you're glad to be on that one today. I can see why you like her so much," she added. "She's good at this kind of thing."

"Yeah, she loves it," I agreed. "She's a lot better of a stock pony than she ever was a show jumper." I glanced back at Misty, who had followed Squib's example and jumped off the bank as well. "Misty, on the other hand..."

AJ grinned. "At least he's good at show jumping."

"Not much use for anything else," I agreed.

"Do you hate him?" AJ asked bluntly.

I shook my head. "No. I used to. Now I just...I don't know. It's not him. I mean, it's not his fault. We're just not a good match, that's all."

"Yeah, I get that." AJ clapped Squib's neck. "I got lucky with this one. What if your mum bought you a different pony? Something straightforward, like Skip, or Lucas?" she asked, naming Susannah and Katy's other ponies. "Think you'd like jumping more then?"

"Maybe. Though it's not just about the jumping," I explained, nudging Rory in the sides with my heels to encourage her to keep up

113

with Squib. "It's being expected to be braver than I am, and feeling like a failure when Misty goes badly because he won so much with Hayley. It's being away from home, missing out on what's happening here because we spend so much time on the road. In some ways, this season has been one of my best so far, just because we've gone to way fewer shows." I cringed at my own words, recollecting why we'd had to cut our season short. "Not that I'm saying it's good, about Hayley…"

"It's okay," AJ assured me. "I know what you mean." She gazed out across the farm thoughtfully. "If I lived here, I might not want to leave either. I'm so jealous of you right now. You have no idea."

We carried on along the top of the rolling hills for some distance. Squib took the lead once more and Misty hurried up to join him, leaving me and Susannah to ride quietly along at the back. The ground dipped down ahead of us, and Katy and AJ disappeared momentarily from sight. Forbes whinnied nervously, wondering where his friends had gone.

"Oh shut up," Susannah told him, then turned to me. "Bet you're not eyeing him up as a new station hack."

I smiled at her. "Not really, no. I'm not sure he's cut out for it. Squib, on the other hand," I said as the dark grey pony reappeared ahead of us on the other side of the dip, still full of energy. "He looks like he could go for days."

"How much further is it?" Susannah asked as I watched Misty bounding up behind Squib, still fighting Katy. Her arms must've been aching like crazy, and I flexed my fingers on Rory's loose reins, feeling the phantom blisters that Katy's ungloved hands were surely developing.

"Not far. See those gates up there?" I pointed a couple of hundred metres ahead to where the track split into three gateways. "We go through the one on the right, and down into that gully."

Stony Flat was just visible in the distance, and I pointed it out to

Susannah as where we were headed.

"And then we have to go all the way back," she said. "No wonder your ponies are so fit."

"We'll go home along the road," I told her. "It's shorter."

"Okay good. I was *not* looking forward to riding down that hill!"

We nudged our ponies up into a trot to catch up to the others, who had stopped at the three gates. AJ twisted in her saddle to look back at me, resting one hand on Squib's round hindquarters.

"Which gate?"

"The one on the right," I told them.

AJ raised her eyebrows. "Sure? It sounds kinda dangerous."

I was confused for a moment, before I saw the old wooden board that was wired to the gate with the name *Shrapnel Valley* painted on it.

"Don't worry. It's perfectly safe," I assured her.

"As long as you promise nobody's going to shoot me," AJ said, leaning forward and unhitching the gate.

"I guarantee it," I replied. "It's just a name, that's all."

We filed through the open gate, and waited while AJ tried to get it latched. Squib wasn't too keen on waiting, and kept jibbing away just as she got close.

"Can I ask why?"

I looked at Susannah. "Why what?"

"Why so many places on your farm are named after battle sites at Gallipoli."

I raised my eyebrows, impressed. "How'd you know that?"

She shrugged. "I did a History essay on it last year. I thought it was a coincidence you're your dad mentioned Walker's Ridge and Quinn's, but then I saw that." She pointed to the sign one of the other gates, identifying it as leading to Lone Pine.

"That one's a misnomer," I told her. "There's got to be close to three hundred pine trees up there now. But yeah, it's a Gallipoli thing. My great-great-grandfather was killed there, and when my great-grandad bought the place and moved onto it, his wife picked names from Gallipoli in memory of her father."

"I like it," Susannah said. "Gives the place a sense of history."

I smiled at her. "I like it too."

AJ finally got the gate latched, and rode over to join us. I surveyed the deep gully that lay ahead in Shrapnel. Steep hills on either side dropped down into a wide gully filled with native trees and bushes, and a small stream, almost dry, trickled along at the bottom. It was a good paddock in these hot conditions, offering plenty of shade and a natural water source, but the sheep had eaten it out and we had to move them before they started destroying the natives.

"Have you guys ever moved sheep before?" They all shook their heads. "The trick is to keep them as relaxed as you can. If you push them too hard, they'll scatter, and the land here's too steep to turn around quickly and get behind them, so if they go every which way, we'll have to start over. Just nudge them along, let them move at their own pace, as long as they're moving and not standing still. But if you can't move one, leave it. It'll find its own way down, or Dad'll pick it up next week."

They all nodded, listening intently as I gave them instructions. It made a refreshing change to be the only one in the group who knew what they were doing. It had never been my role before, but it was surprisingly easy to take charge.

"AJ, you go along the ridgeline to the right. This gully's just over a kilometre long, and about three-quarters of the way along you'll see a corrugated iron shed at the bottom by the stream. Follow the track down to it, then ride downstream until you get to the gate. Open it all the way on its hinges and hook it back to the fence, then ride back the way you came. Katy, you go left. There's more bush on your side so I'll send Cave that way to flush the sheep out. Make your way down the slope on an angle, aim to get to the bottom about halfway along. Susannah and I will come at the back and keep them bunched up as much as we can, hopefully with Thor's help. Any questions?"

AJ raised her hand immediately. "What do we do if the sheep start stampeding?"

"They're sheep," I told her. "They're going to run away from you, not at you."

"Hear that, Forbes?" Susannah asked her pony. "Sheep are not dangerous."

"He doesn't believe you," Katy said with a smirk as I whistled up the dogs. They both came running in, ready to work, and I dropped the dog whistle from my mouth and let it hang around my neck again.

"Okay, let's move out. AJ, trot along the ridge where you can, but go slowly down into the valley or you'll spook the sheep back in our direction. Once the gate's open, stick to a walk. That goes for the rest of us as well. Slow and steady gets it done."

AJ headed off as instructed, Squib trotting purposefully forward across the brittle grass with his head held high. Misty jibbed and cantered on the spot, furious at being left behind, and I told Katy to start him off along her side of the ridge.

"Keep him as slow as you can. There's a reason we don't usually use him to move stock," I said and she grinned.

"Yes boss. C'mon Misty, let's go."

I watched them go, sitting still in Rory's saddle as Forbes fidgeted at her side and the dogs waited impatiently in front of me, their eyes fixed on my face. I gave AJ and Katy a moment to get ahead of us, then sent the dogs away. They split off in their respective directions, Cave going left as instructed, and Thor heading to the right, both in full bark. I nudged Rory into a walk as sheep started moving down the hill. Thor was still green, and was moving too fast, flushing out as many sheep as he could without paying attention to where they were headed.

117

"Thor, go back!" I called to him. He slowed down and looked at me, then came jogging back towards me. "Keep out," I reminded him, and he extended the arc of his circle, sweeping wider around the side of the hill and moving the sheep a little more slowly.

Cave worked his side of the hill diligently, barking insistently at sheep that weren't sure they wanted to move. He was an excellent working dog, but he had a tendency to get fixated on one or two sheep that wouldn't move at the speed he deemed appropriate, instead of keeping an eye on the bigger picture. I told Susannah to stay straight, and rode Rory up behind the huddle of stubborn ewes to help Cave out. The sight of Rory approaching changed their stubborn minds, and they started shuffling grumpily down the hill.

"Come by, Cave, come by," I called him and he got back to work, sweeping higher along the top of the ridge without having to be told.

I turned my head to check on Thor, locating him quickly partway down his side of the hill. He slid down a steep bank on his belly, barking loudly at a knot of sheep, which scattered in all directions, including directly towards Forbes, who was on his own in the middle of the gully. Terrified, Forbes froze, his feet planted and eyes popping, every nerve on edge.

I whistled to Thor, sending him back around behind the sheep to move them down. He obeyed, gathering the sheep quickly and barking them back down. But Thor's enthusiasm was his undoing as he failed to give the sheep time to gather their thoughts and they went into panic mode, running directly past Forbes and brushing against his legs in their desperation to get away from the barking dog.

Forbes snorted and spun around, coming face-to-face with the last sheep in the bunch, which tried to avoid him by leaping sideways. Unfortunately the hill was too steep and the ewe couldn't get purchase on it. After a quick scrabble, she lost her footing and tumbled back down onto the path, landing right in front of Forbes and still rolling in his direction.

The dark bay pony had had enough. He leapt into the air, clearing the sheep that was tumbling downhill beneath his hooves, bucked hard on landing and took off back up the hill towards the gate. I watched him go, Susannah still in the saddle but without her stirrups, struggling to pull him up and turn him around. I sent Thor back up onto his side of the ridge, keeping a close eye on him, and he settled into his work better after that. Susannah soon reappeared, shaking her head in disgust.

"Yeah, I definitely don't want him for stock work," I told her as I rode Rory back down to join her.

"Good thing he can jump," she muttered. "Or he'd be completely worthless."

We rode slowly down the gully, pausing regularly to let the dogs push the sheep on ahead of us. Forbes clung closely to Rory's side, whinnying nervously whenever she left him to go and help the dogs, but not having any more sheep-induced panic attacks. I spotted Misty making his way along the side of the hill ahead of us, his jig-jogging finally ceased now that he was on his own and not part of a group. He was as fiercely independent as his owner, and I wondered again how Hayley was doing. A quick check of my watch revealed that her surgery should be underway by now, and I closed my eyes and prayed that it was going well.

"Uh, Tess?"

I opened my eyes to see sheep scattering back towards us at speed. The dogs came bounding down the hill to hold them without needing instruction, but the sheep were nervous, and the dogs had limited success. It took me a moment to work out what'd spooked them, until I heard hoof beats moving rapidly in our direction. I stood up in my stirrups, trying to see through the increasingly thick scrub. I had eyes on Misty, so I knew it must be Squib, but I couldn't work out what AJ was thinking until her pony came into view.

She wasn't on him.

10

FULL CIRCLE

Fortunately, Squib stopped when he saw us, and I was able to catch him and lead him back down the gully once the dogs had the sheep moving again. We found AJ with Katy, nursing her shoulder but insisting that she was fine. Apparently Squib had bucked her off when a sheep had jumped out from behind a tree and startled him, which I think made Susannah feel better about her own pony's shortcomings.

"They're not all cut out for the farm life," I agreed as AJ remounted. "You can stay down a bit lower now, we'll just push these ones along and gather up whatever's left on the way. The rest will work it out eventually."

We rode on down towards the gate, and I moved AJ and Katy into flanking positions while the dogs kept the sheep moving forward. The natural terrain funnelled them effectively through the gap, and once they realised that they were going to greener pastures, they picked up speed and made their way willingly onto Stony Flat.

As the last ewe jogged through the gate, I rode up to AJ.

"What's your count?"

She looked surprised. "I…was I supposed to be counting?"

I turned towards Katy, who seemed equally surprised, and shook her head.

"Okay. Never mind."

We left the gate open behind us and rode down towards the old wooden stockyards that sat under a stand of willow trees alongside the dusty farm road. The dogs and ponies drank thirstily from a nearby trough while I dismounted and walked through the yards, checking for loose or broken boards, making sure that the gates still swung on their hinges and latched where they were supposed to. There were a few things there to fix, but nothing that would take more than half a day at most. So that was some good news that I could take home to Dad.

The girls had all dismounted and were stretching their legs while their ponies munched on the longer grass in this paddock.

"I'm going to be so sore tonight," AJ lamented. "Six weeks without riding did not prepare me for this."

"Same," Susannah agreed, wincing as she adjusted her designer breeches. "I think my butt is rubbed raw."

Katy just shook her head at them both. "You two are pathetic. Hey Tess, tell me that shed there's got a toilet."

"There's a long drop out the back," I confirmed. "Not sure anyone's used it in a year or more, but help yourself."

Katy pulled a face. "Okay, no thanks. I'll just go find some long grass to pee in."

She headed off around behind the stockyards, while Susannah fidgeted awkwardly. After grumbling to herself about having drunk way too much water, she left me holding Forbes and went off to answer the call of nature herself.

AJ grinned as she watched her go. "Bet you anything she's never done that before," she commented, then laughed at my expression. "Seriously. It'll be good for her though. Toughen her up a bit."

"She's not so bad, when you get to know her," I said idly as Katy reappeared from behind the shed and pointed Susannah in an appropriate direction.

"No, she's not," AJ agreed. "None of us are, I hope."

I looked over at her. "Course not."

"You're so different out here," AJ commented, as Katy paused to pat the dogs on her way past them.

"Me?"

"Yeah. You're like, confident. Relaxed. In control." She grinned at me. "I'm not used to seeing that side of you, but I like it."

"Well that's because you normally only see me when I'm crapping myself about having to ride Misty," I told her. "Give me a reliable pony and a proper job to do and it's cake."

"You sure make it look that way," AJ replied. "I'm glad I came along. I like this Tess. She's a bad-ass."

I blushed and turned away as Katy came back over to us, taking Misty's reins from her friend and giving him a hug around the neck. Before I could warn her, Misty had dipped his head and nipped her sharply on the hip, making her yelp.

"He does that," I told her as she pulled her shirt up to reveal an oncoming bruise. "He didn't draw blood though. He must like you."

Once Susannah had returned, I whistled up the dogs and clapped Rory on her sweaty neck before swinging back up into the saddle.

"Homeward bound," I told the others as they remounted, groaning and complaining as they did so. "And don't worry, we'll go the shortest way so you can all still walk in the morning."

"Bit late for that," groaned Susannah as Forbes broke into a job.

We rode back across Stony Flat towards the road gate. Squib took the lead once more, and I let Rory walk out with her reins loose, taking her time. I stood in my stirrups as I rode, trying to count up the sheep to get an approximate idea of how many we'd brought down, although I wasn't sure how big the mob was supposed to be anyway. Then AJ's call attracted my attention.

"Tess! The gate's locked."

"What?" I kicked Rory into a trot and hurried up to them. "It shouldn't be…oh." AJ was right. A thick metal chain was wrapped around the gatepost, and a heavy padlock hung from it.

"Tell me you have a key," Susannah said, but I shook my head.

"Not on me. I didn't think we'd need it. Dad doesn't usually lock the gates off the access routes, just off the main road. But there were some cattle thefts last year, and he must've come back and locked up anything with direct access." I shook my head. "Crap."

"*Please* tell me this doesn't mean we have to go all the way back the way we came."

"Well, no," I told Susannah. "We could go home through the pines instead of riding down the switchback. Other than that, though…"

"Can't we just jump the gate?" AJ asked. "It's not that high. These ponies can all clear it easily."

Their eyes were all on me, and I swallowed nervously, seeking desperately for an excuse. "Um, I don't know if Rory will. She's pretty tired and I haven't jumped her in months."

"You'll be fine," Katy insisted. "She'll only get more tired going back that other way, and you've done loads of metre-tens on her in the past, I've seen you. This gate's nowhere near that. Just sit down and kick on. C'mon, Misty will give you all a lead."

I watched as Katy shortened her reins and sent Misty forward into a canter. He was still full of energy, and he raced eagerly towards the gate, sized it up and flung himself over. I'd known he would go – Hayley had a bad habit of jumping fences and gates all across the farm, and chances were he'd jumped this one before. Squib followed suit, with Forbes, terrified of being left behind, right on his heels. They both landed safely and pulled up as the dogs slipped through the fence and lay in the long grass on the other side.

I shortened my reins and took a deep breath. *You can do this.* I nudged Rory into a trot, then into a canter. She was lethargic, and I dug my heels into her sides as we turned towards the gate. It looked immense, no more jumpable than a ten foot wall, and I was paralysed by doubt. Rory cantered towards it, then slowed down uncertainly. Katy was yelling at me to kick her on, but Rory's hesitation had jangled my nerves, and she dribbled to a pathetic halt in front of it.

"Do you want me to have a go?" Katy offered, but I shook my head, furious with myself. *I like this Tess. She's bad-ass.* Time to prove AJ right, instead of proving her wrong.

I turned Rory around and gave her a sharp kick. Startled, she leapt into a canter and I rode a wide circle, then aimed her at the gate. This time I stopped looking at the obstacle. I sat down in the saddle, clamped my legs around Rory's sides and looked at the faces of my friends on the other side of the gate. Rory cleared it in a smooth arc, and I was grinning with relief as we landed.

"See? Easy," Katy declared as Misty swung left, heading home.

The ponies strolled up the road, even Squib's walk having slowed slightly after several hours of work. The dogs jogged ahead of us, lying down occasionally to wait for us to catch up, then trotting on. The sun baked down, making Susannah complain that she'd forgotten her sunblock and was going to be burned to a crisp in the morning. Katy took her helmet off and shook out her sweaty hair until Misty shied at a pothole and she hastily put it back on. AJ sat sideways in her saddle, one leg hooked over the pommel and her stirrups dangling against Squib's round sides as she chatted to us behind her. The road stretched out ahead of us, shimmering in the hot afternoon sun, and I leaned forward and wrapped my arms around Rory's neck, my cheek pressed against her sweat-encrusted coat.

"You're the best," I told her, and she bobbed her head agreeably.

We were both tired, and I closed my eyes and let her smooth, relaxed stride lull me as we walked on and on down the road.

"Are you asleep?"

"Yes," I told Susannah, then winced as her metal stirrup collided with my ankle yet again when Forbes shot sideways into Rory.

My patient pony swished her tail and pulled a face at Forbes, but he was distracted by the monstrous irrigators in the crop paddocks across the road, which had just turned on. I tilted my wrist and checked the time – it was later than I thought.

"We should get a move on," I told the others, stretching my back muscles as I sat up. I was out of shape as well, but I wasn't going to admit it. "Anyone's pony got energy left for cantering?"

It was a rhetorical question, really. Squib and Misty were dead set on racing all the way home, Forbes was desperate to escape from the ticking irrigators, and even Rory picked up the pace when she thought she was being left behind. We let the ponies canter down the side of the road, jumping back and forth across the drainage ditches to amuse ourselves as we went. And I finally, finally felt comfortable in the saddle again.

Eventually we eased to a trot, and then back to a walk, patting our blowing ponies.

"Squib's going to sleep well tonight," AJ declared, clapping his neck. "We need to do this again sometime." Her eyes lit up as she turned towards me. "Can we camp out overnight?"

Susannah looked startled, but Katy was immediately keen. "Yes! After Horse of the Year. Let's do it. Ride all day and sleep out under the stars – it'll be perfect!"

I nodded slowly, thinking. "Yeah, we could do that. If we rode the fences right out to the south boundary it'd take us most of the day, and we could camp there. There's an old dairy shed in one of those back paddocks that we could sleep in if we needed shelter."

AJ scoffed. "No way. No tents either, we've gotta build a campfire and hunt and gather our food…" She rambled on as Susannah looked increasingly alarmed by her propositions.

"If you want to go full paleo, you go right ahead," I told AJ. "But I'm bringing food, and a gas stove, and possibly a tent. We could always drive out there the day before and leave our gear, so we wouldn't have to carry much with us."

"That sounds like heaven. I'm *so* in," AJ said. "What about it, Susannah? You game?"

She nodded. "Sure, why not? Although I might bring Skip next time, if Dad will let me," she decided as Forbes took exception to Thor crossing the road in front of him and shied into Rory for what must've been the tenth time at least. "Oof, sorry Tess! Honestly, Forbes, would you get a grip?"

"It's okay. And you can always borrow Misty," I offered, laughing at the expression on her face. "Or we've got a few farm hacks that are pretty solid, but I can't promise you'll get the smoothest ride."

"She'll be fine, she just needs to harden up," Katy said dismissively. "And don't think you can back out of it, Susannah Andrews. We'll drag you here kicking and screaming if we have to."

AJ turned in her saddle and grinned at us. "Isn't friendship great?"

"How much further is it?" Katy asked, trying to slow Misty's quickening stride. He yanked at the bit, resuming his jig-jogging, much to Katy's obvious irritation. "Oh Misty don't, you've given me stitch already."

"He knows we're nearly back," I told her. "It's not far, just under a k from here. You might want to get off and lead him though, because he won't quit jogging now."

Katy groaned and kicked her feet out of the stirrups, jumping to the ground while Misty jigged along the road. He turned his head and looked at her in surprise, then bunted her firmly with his head, knocking her sideways almost into the ditch.

"There's a pony up there," AJ told me, looking ahead to where a scruffy black pony was munching grass on the side of the road.

"Yeah, that's…" My voice broke off as Susannah interrupted. She was looking ahead to Jonty's cottage, where we could see his mother hanging washing on their clothesline. Murray was grazing in the front yard.

"Does someone actually *live* there?" she asked, sounding slightly horrified. I glanced at her, but she didn't notice, her eyes fixed on Jonty's mum. I was glad he was still out fixing fences, although I felt a little ashamed to even be thinking that.

"Oh I know where we are now," AJ said. "We drove past that place when we came in. It's not far from here at all."

"Thank God," Katy grumbled as Misty dragged her down the road, and I wondered if she was regretting her decision to dismount.

We came closer to the cottage, and I started asking Susannah about how her pony Buck was enjoying his recent retirement. She warmed immediately to the subject and was sufficiently distracted, focusing her attention on me and away from the shabby cottage. Over her shoulder, I saw a face appear in the front window. It disappeared again, and moments later the front door swung open and Phoebe appeared on the front step, watching us ride by. AJ waved to her, and she waved back, then came down the steps and limped barefoot across their raggedy lawn.

"Hi Tess," she called, beaming at me, and I smiled back.

"Hi Phoebe. What've you done to your foot?"

She stopped at the fence, putting one hand on it to balance herself as she turned her left foot over and showed me a dirty bandage on the sole.

"I cut it. Wanna see?" she offered, her fingers already picking at the edge of it.

"No, I'm good," I told her, and she shrugged, as though it was my loss.

Taniwha looked up as we approached, his ears pricked up with vague interest at the newcomers. Squib, who was as sociable as his owner, bustled over to meet him, but Misty continued to tow Katy down the road, and Susannah didn't seem inclined to pause. I waved briefly to Phoebe as we passed, and she leaned on the wooden fence and watched us ride by, her unbrushed hair hanging loose on her bony shoulders.

We rode on, the ponies all disinclined to stop now that they were so close to home, except for Squib, who was still hanging back chatting to Taniwha. I looked over my shoulder to check on AJ as we carried on up the road, and saw that she'd ridden over to Phoebe and was letting her pat Squib's broad face. I leaned a hand on Rory's rump and smiled as I watched them, still listening with half an ear to Susannah's description of Buck's lung infection.

"Here comes trouble," Katy called, and I looked forward to see Jonty walking up the road towards us. The dogs shot forward to meet him, barking an enthusiastic greeting and startling Forbes yet again.

"Slow learner, isn't he?" I commented to Susannah as AJ bid Phoebe farewell and trotted on up the road to re-join us.

"I really thought he'd have settled down by now," she complained. "If this is what he's going to be like when I take him out and show him the world, maybe I'll just keep him at home."

Katy had stopped to talk to Jonty, and we all drew to a halt behind her as he let Misty rub his sweaty head on his shoulder. His eyes flickered over to me and his smile widened as I grinned back at him.

"Good ride? Nobody fell off?"

We all looked at AJ, who rolled her eyes. "Only once," she reminded us. "And I'm fine. No harm, no foul."

"Where're you going?" Katy asked him, fending off Misty's attempts to nip her and get her moving again.

Jonty nodded up the road towards the cottage, and I knew all was about to be revealed. "Home."

"Oh," AJ said awkwardly, then pointed behind us to Phoebe, who was still leaning on the front fence. "Is that your sister? She's sweet."

"Yeah. And she's a demon really," Jonty said with a grin as Katy spun around and stared back down the road.

"Wait, was that your old pony back there?"

"Yeah, that's Taniwha. You remember him?"

Katy nodded. "I *thought* he looked familiar. He's got that chunk missing out of his ear, for one, and honestly there's no other pony on earth that's *that* ugly."

"Katy!" AJ said in horror, but Jonty just laughed.

"It's okay, he knows. I tell him every night before bed."

"Did you get the fences done?" I asked him, wanting to change the subject.

Jonty nodded. "Yep, all sorted. I'll let you guys carry on," he added as Misty spun around impatiently, making Katy dance sideways to prevent him crushing her toes. "See you all later." They said their goodbyes as Jonty walked up to Rory and put a hand on my knee. "You doing okay?"

And just like that, everything I'd been trying not to think about all day came flooding back into my mind. When I was with my friends, I could make myself forget about Hayley, and her surgery, and everything that might go wrong, and all of the possible verdicts that we didn't want to hear. They didn't know, not really, not the full story. But Jonty did.

I shrugged, fighting back the sudden threat of tears. "I'm good."

His fingers closed around my knee and I laid my hand on top of his. "You want me to come back up tonight and help feed out?" he asked.

I nodded. "If you don't mind."

"Not at all." He gave my leg a last gentle squeeze, then slid his hand out from under mine. "I'll see you in a couple hours."

"Okay."

With a last brief wave, Jonty headed towards home. I sat in Rory's saddle and watched him, the late afternoon sun glinting off his dark hair. Phoebe came hobbling to meet him, and he swung her up onto his back and piggybacked her back to their house, tossing her up and down as he went. Her happy squeals followed us as we carried on down the road.

We rode in silence for a moment, then AJ spoke. "I had no idea."

She looked guilty, but not as much as Susannah, who spoke next. "I'm sorry too. I wouldn't have said that, if I knew..."

"It's fine," I said, not wanting to have a conversation about it. "It is what it is."

"Is that why your mum doesn't like him?" AJ asked, and I nodded, then shrugged.

"It's part of it."

"I can't believe he's still got that pony," Katy mused, walking along at Misty's shoulder with one arm resting on the saddle flap. "God, it's ugly."

"You're ugly," AJ told her, nudging her sharply in the shoulder with the toe of her boot.

Katy stuck her tongue out at her, then turned around and walked backwards, looking at me.

"So Tess, riddle me this. How does someone who learned to ride on *that*," she asked, pointing back towards Taniwha, "get good enough to be able to ride *this*?" and she motioned at Misty, who was tugging irritably at the bit.

I shrugged, but AJ and Susannah were looking at me equally intently, as curious as Katy was.

"You must have *some* idea," Susannah asked, looking back over her shoulder at the cottage.

"I told you he used to ride for Ken Hobson," I reminded Katy, and she pulled a face.

"Yeah, but when I realised out who he was, I figured that there must be more to it than that. Ken's rough as guts," she explained to the others. "Get breakers off the track and horses off the dog man and rehabs them to sell on. Or he drugs them and sells them on, according to some people. The least reputable horse dealer in Hawke's Bay, and he can't ride for shit. Jonty might've learned how to stick on from being there, but how'd he learn to school a horse properly and ride as well as he does?"

"He managed it somehow," I insisted, despite her sceptical expression. "That's what he tells me, and he swears it's true."

Katy just shook her head. "Well if that's the case, then he's got some serious natural talent." Her eyes lingered on Taniwha, grazing peacefully in the long grass. "Shame to see it going to waste."

She turned around and walked forwards again, tugging sharply at Misty's reins. I glanced over my shoulder and took a last look at the cottage before we turned the corner and it disappeared from sight.

11

FIST FIGHT

I led Rory back to her paddock and slipped her halter off as Katy's truck drove out of our yard. Copper whinnied a welcome and came trotting over to see Rory, but she seemed unimpressed by his affection, and started immediately grazing while he walked in a circle around her. I shut the gate and leaned on it, my body tired and aching from the long day's ride. I was glad my friends had come, but I was also glad they'd gone. The brief respite from reality that had accompanied them was over, and the real world was about to come crashing back in. It was just after four in the afternoon, which meant that Hayley's surgery had to be over by now. The window they'd given for how long it might take was well and truly closed, and somewhere, that information was waiting for me to learn it.

I couldn't put it off any longer. I pushed myself off the gate, hooked Rory's halter over the gate post and walked up towards the woolshed, looking for my father. He wasn't there, but Hugh greeted me with a smile.

He wouldn't be smiling if anything was wrong, I told myself as he came towards me.

"Looking for your dad?" I nodded, and he pointed towards the homestead. "Just went down there looking for you, I reckon."

"Okay."

I waited for him to say something else, anything really, but he just went back to what he was doing. My stomach was clenching in on itself, and I felt weirdly numb, like a zombie as I walked down towards the house. I walked back past the horse paddock, and for the first time in my life, I wished that Misty was there. His absence suddenly seemed like a bad omen, because we all knew that Hayley loved that pony more than anything or anyone else in the world. I wondered how I'd never appreciated that before, and a surge of guilt passed over me as I remembered the countless arguments we'd had about selling him, sending him away and out of our care. Even though Hayley was the one who had suggested that Katy take him, I couldn't shake the image in my head of Misty on our ride today, a ride that had seemed like so much fun at the time. But looking back, I wasn't sure that Misty had really enjoyed it. I pictured him as he'd been by the end, when all the other ponies had been walking calmly on a loose rein, but Misty was still surging and straining against the bridle, sweat pouring in dark rivulets down his face as he towed Katy on foot back down the road.

For the first time in days, I imagined myself on his back. Imagined his hard, muscled neck in front of me, his curved ears always fixed forward, his entire body pumping with energy. There had been bad times, scary times, times when he'd frustrated the hell out of me, times when I'd been certain that he hated me as much as I loathed him, but there had also been brief flashes of brilliance. When I'd pushed myself to get over my fear and had jumped my first clear round on him, when we'd won the Pony Grand Prix at Taupo, when we'd raced Jonty and Copper all the way up to Lone Pine and left them in our dust. We'd ridden home along the dirt road that evening as an incredible sunset painted the sky with a deep orange glow, and Misty had walked calmly on a slack rein, swinging his head from side to side to take in the scenery, none of us in any great rush to get home.

It was strange, the way I suddenly missed him. He'd only been gone five minutes, but already I missed his presence. I missed the spark in his dark eyes, the way he'd sneak mouthfuls of my hair when he thought I wasn't paying attention, or nuzzle at my hip then deliver a sharp nip before looking away as though he was perfectly innocent. The paddock looked empty without him in it, and I was suddenly reminded of the old saying that my Pop used to come up with all the time.

You don't know what you've got 'til it's gone.

Dad stepped out onto the porch as I approached the house, and my eyes flew to his face, trying to read his emotions. I broke into a run, hurrying to meet him, my feet feeling as though they were barely touching the ground.

"Have you heard anything? Is she okay?"

Dad shrugged, shaking his head slightly. I came to a sudden halt, overwhelmed with emotion, and he moved quickly towards me.

"Sorry, I didn't mean…I don't know. The surgeon's flight out of Melbourne was delayed, so they pushed the surgery back several hours. She's still waiting to go in."

My knees felt weak, and Dad's hands gripped my shoulders, holding me steady.

"Sorry. I didn't mean to scare you."

I punched him feebly in the chest. "Don't do that."

"Sorry," he said for the third time, pulling me in towards him and kissing my forehead. "So far as I know, she's doing okay. Hungry, apparently," he added, and I found myself smiling. "Hasn't eaten in almost a day."

"Poor Mum." Hayley was never fun to be around when she was hungry. I could only imagine how vile she was being to Mum, being starved and stressed all at once. "But they're still going to do it today?"

"As soon as the surgeon's finished with his prior patient," Dad assured me with a heavy sigh. "It's just a waiting game right now."

I looked up at his weatherworn face. The stress was visible in his eyes, and I wrapped my arms around him and gave him a hug. He hugged me back tightly, making it difficult to breathe, but I didn't mind. After a long moment, he released me.

"Better get back into it," he said. "Hugh still up the yards?"

"Yep."

"Righto."

"D'you want some help?" I offered. "I can come up if you want, do…whatever."

"Nah, you're all right. Stick around here in case your mum rings back, eh?"

"Yeah, of course."

He nodded and started to walk away, then turned back. "How'd you get on moving the draft mob?"

"Good. We forgot to count them," I admitted, but he waved that off as inconsequential.

"We'll do that in a couple days. They looking all right though, all in good nick?"

"Yeah, not bad," I told him. "And the yards are okay too, nothing a hammer and nails and a bit of CRC won't fix."

"Cheers," Dad said. "Appreciate it."

"No problem."

He cast his eyes up towards the horse paddock, where Copper and Rory were just visible as shapes on the side of the hill.

"Misty get away all right?"

"Yep."

I pushed down my reservations. Hayley wanted him to go to Katy. She wanted him to show jump, and I couldn't ride him, so someone had to. Another flash of memory, this time of riding Misty in the paddock here at home, circling him at a canter, his jaw relaxed against the bit, his body flexed around my leg, his rhythm steady and controlled. I'd felt as though I could jump the moon, and as I walked into the house, I wondered if I would ever ride a pony like him again.

I made a beef casserole for dinner, but Mum rang right before we sat down to eat it to say that Hayley was finally going in for surgery, so I don't think Dad or I tasted it. He went into the lounge and turned the TV on while I cleared up and then went to my room to get started on my homework. For once in my life I welcomed the distraction and the concentration it required, throwing myself into my studies with unprecedented dedication. I spent hours going through every subject, searching for any unfinished work, looking up any upcoming assignments that I could start working on or researching. But eventually, as the clock passed eleven, I ran out of work. I lay down on my bed, fully dressed, and scrolled through Facebook on my phone, but nothing interesting was happening. My eyelids got heavier and heavier, and I closed my eyes, just for a moment...

I was almost asleep when the phone rang. I jerked upright, inadvertently kicking Colin who was sneakily sleeping on my bed because Mum wasn't home and Dad hadn't noticed. He yelped, and I told him to shush and stay in my room while I hurried down the hall, the ringing phone reverberating in my ears. Then it stopped.

"Hello?"

I stopped in the doorway of the lounge, my heart pounding so hard that I could barely hear anything. I watched Dad's face for clues, watched him close his eyes and lean forward, elbows on his knees, and for a moment the whole world spun. Then my father leaned back against the couch cushions, passed a hand over his eyes, and smiled.

"That's good news."

I don't remember deciding to move, but suddenly I was standing in front of my father, and he held his arms out to me, cradling the phone between his ear and his shoulder. I went willingly into his embrace, feeling the security of his arm around me as I leaned up against him, tucking my legs underneath me as I heard my mother's voice on the other end of the line.

"…confident they got all of it. They need to do more tests, of course, but they say they're very hopeful."

"That's great," Dad said again, seemingly lost for any other words.

"Is she awake?" I whispered to him, and he repeated my question to Mum.

"She was, right afterwards, and she knew her name and what had happened, and her speech was normal, so that's all good," Mum said, sounding tearful and shaken. "I just want to bring her home."

I closed my eyes as they finished their brief conversation before Mum went back to sit vigil beside Hayley's bed. Dad put the cordless phone on the couch next to him and sighed, then gave me a firm hug with both arms.

"You should get back to bed," he told me. "You've got school in the morning."

"No I don't," I reminded him. "It's Sunday tomorrow." I looked up at the clock on the mantelpiece and corrected myself. "Well, today."

"Right." He rubbed his eyes, then reached forward and picked up the TV remote from the coffee table, using it to shut off the soccer game he'd been pretending to watch. "Well, I'm bushed. Time for bed, eh?"

We stood up, and so did Colin, who was waiting for me in the doorway. He slunk backwards into the hall as Dad caught sight of him.

"What's that mongrel doing in the house?"

"Keeping me company," I said, looking up at him. "I won't tell if you won't."

Dad sighed, then nodded. "Just for tonight."

"Thanks Dad." I went out into the hall, catching a last glimpse of Colin's tail disappearing into my bedroom. "Night."

I woke in a tangle of sweat and blankets. I'd overslept, and the sun was beaming through the curtains that I'd forgotten to close, heating my room like an oven. Throwing my covers off, I opened the windows wide before heading down to the kitchen. The door to my parents' bedroom was open, and I smiled at Dad's awkward attempt to make the bed.

Colin padded down the hall behind me then ran to the front door and whined, so I let him out and he ran off across the lawn to relieve himself. I filled a glass of water from the tap and stood in front of the kitchen sink, looking out across the farm. It was a bright, shining morning, the perfect kind of weather for a day when things were finally starting to feel right. I was halfway through my second glass of water when the front door swung open, and Dad stuck his head in and bellowed.

"TESS!"

I jumped, sloshing water down the front of my t-shirt, and turned around.

"I'm here," I told him, dabbing at my shirt with a tea towel.

"We need you up at the yards. We're short-handed and need to get the beef weaners ready for the sale on Tuesday."

Business as usual, then.

"Okay." I poured the rest of the water out and set the glass on the draining board. "I can run down and see if Jonty's free to help us as well," I offered, trying to keep my voice casual. "I'm sure he wouldn't mind lending a hand."

"He's already up at the cattle yards," Dad told me. "Unlike someone I know, he actually got out of bed before the sun was all the way up."

"I'll be there in a minute," I promised, grabbing a banana out of the fruit bowl and hurrying back to my room to get dressed.

I could hear the weaner calves well before I could see them, yelling for their mothers who were suddenly out of their sight for the first time. Some of the cows were bellowing back as Gordy, Jock and a team of dogs moved them up the raceway towards new pasture, but several of them were moving eagerly, unfazed about leaving their children behind. We usually didn't wean the calves this early, but with the drought showing no sign of ending soon and Hayley's medical bills quickly piling up, Dad had decided to destock as much as possible before the cattle lost condition. Weaners were going for high prices to other parts of the country that weren't as dry as Hawke's Bay, and rumour had it that there were a few keen buyers coming from up north to the sales at Stortford Lodge tomorrow morning. It was one of the more unpleasant inevitabilities of farming that you couldn't keep every animal you bred, and it was better to sell them to someone who had better feed conditions than try to run too many cattle on dry pasture. I knew all of that, but it didn't mean I had to like it.

The calves were larger and more difficult to handle than the sheep, but the work was running steadily and relatively smoothly. Jonty was working at the other end of the yards with Bayard, pushing the calves up into the race in small groups to where Dad and Hugh were evaluating them one-by-one, checking their condition and general health, and deciding which ones to keep and breed from next season. It was slow, methodical work, and pretty soon my inadequate breakfast was telling on me, making my stomach rumble. Dad and Hugh didn't seem to be in any hurry, deliberating for quite some time over a particular heifer that Hugh liked the look of but Dad wasn't sure about.

"You can't sell them all," Hugh told him as Dad shook his head and sent the heifer into the sale pen. "You need to keep some stock for next season."

"Not if it doesn't rain," Dad grumbled. "I'm not keeping cows around just to starve them."

Hugh shrugged, accepting the argument as lost before checking his watch. "Reckon it's time for smoko."

"What's your problem, man?"

I straightened up and turned off the tap, dropping the hose onto the ground. It was past midday and we'd only just stopped for lunch. My wet hair dripped down my neck, soaking the collar of my shirt, but I paid no attention to it. I'd never heard Jonty raise his voice like that before, but I had a hunch who he was talking to.

"There's no problem." Bayard's voice was low, almost a mumble.

But Jonty didn't believe him, and frankly, neither did I.

"Bull. This is about Tess, isn't it?"

I didn't blame him for being annoyed. Bayard had spent the entire morning telling Jonty that he was doing everything wrong, constantly nagging at him and making a point about how much faster he was at drenching the calves. Jonty was a quick learner and had been trying hard, but Bayard hadn't let up, even when Hugh had told him to. I could tell that the constant criticism was getting on Jonty's nerves, and I hoped Dad would have the sense to separate them this afternoon.

"Tess isn't the problem, you are," Bayard told him. "You need to stay away from her."

I rolled my eyes and straightened up, about to step in and tell the pair of them to get over themselves, but Jonty spoke before I could.

"Don't you think Tess should make that decision for herself?"

Bayard gave a bitter laugh. "Tess doesn't know what I know about you. If she did, she wouldn't touch you with a ten-foot pole."

"She already knows, mate. I told her about it ages ago, after the last time you tried it on with this crap."

There was a pause as Bayard clearly took in the shocking revelation that I actually had faith in my boyfriend.

"She's only heard your side," he tried, but Jonty just laughed over him.

"Whose side do you suggest she listens to?" he asked. "Yours? Look, I've done things I'm not proud of. We all have. But if you're going to keep making a big deal out of something that you don't understand, maybe you should consider that there's things I know about *you* that you wouldn't want me to tell anyone."

Now it was Bayard's turn to sound alarmed. "What are you talking about?"

Jonty lowered his voice slightly, and I leaned closer, feeling guilty for eavesdropping, but unable to prevent myself from the temptation.

"I'm talking about Hayley's party. I know where you went after dark, and I know who you were with."

There was a silence, then a crash as the wall of the woolshed shook. I couldn't stay hidden any longer, and quickly stepped around the corner to see Jonty with his back up against the woolshed and Bayard's fist on its way towards his face.

"Stop it!" I cried, and Bayard's head turned towards me even as he followed through with his punch.

Jonty ducked, and Bayard's fist hit the corrugated iron, making him wince, then he gasped as Jonty landed a punch of his own to Bayard's stomach. Blood was running freely from a cut high on Jonty's cheekbone, and he stepped back with his hands held up in surrender.

"You got the wrong idea, man," he said. "I wasn't saying…"

But Bayard didn't listen. He went in for a second punch, pulling his arm right back and then jabbing forward. Jonty saw it coming and blocked it, wincing slightly as Bayard's fist hit his forearm but countering with a sharp jab of his own, straight into Bayard's nose. It started gushing blood, and I yelled at them again.

"STOP IT! BOTH OF YOU!"

They ignored me. Bayard was lunging at Jonty now, tackling him to the ground, and I knew that he was counting on his strength to pin Jonty down and pummel him. Panicking, I did the only thing left I could think of.

"DAD!" I shouted as loud as I could, running towards them and jumping on Bayard's back, locking my arms around his neck. "Stop it!"

I grabbed a fistful of his thick blonde hair in one hand and pulled it as hard as I could. Bayard jerked backwards and twisted his shoulders, trying to throw me off him, and then I heard more voices shouting, and footsteps running towards us.

"Hey!" Hugh yelled at them. "What the hell are you lot playin' at?"

A hand grabbed Bayard's shirt collar and dragged him to his feet as I relinquished my hold on him and staggered backwards, my heart racing. Hugh had a firm grip on Bayard while Dad stood between the boys with his arms folded, glaring at them both in disgust.

Jonty pushed himself into a sitting position, his cheek still bleeding profusely and one eye starting to swell shut.

Dad glanced at him. "Get up."

Jonty scrambled to his feet, his dark hair falling into nervous eyes. I took an instinctive step towards him, but Dad lifted his hand and shook his head at me. I stopped, and he looked at the boys, every line of his body locked in furious tension.

"Who's going to tell me what in blazes that was about?" he asked.

Jonty looked at Bayard, who said nothing. Blood dripped from his chin and onto the dirt at his feet.

"You going to answer me?" Dad asked, looking first at Jonty, who looked at the ground, then to Bayard, who shook his head. "Then get out of my sight, the pair of you." Jonty lifted his head again in dismay, but he didn't speak.

"NOW!" Dad snapped. "And I don't want to see either one of you back on my property until you're prepared to give me a damned good explanation for what just happened."

Jonty didn't even look at me, just turned away and started walking down the driveway with slumped shoulders. Hugh grabbed Bayard by the chin and looked at his still bleeding nose, then shoved him towards the woolshed, telling him to get cleaned up before he got in the ute.

"Bayard started it," I told Dad.

He frowned at me. "I didn't ask you."

"I'm telling you," I said. "I heard the whole thing. It wasn't Jonty's fault."

"I'm not overly interested in whose fault it was, or who punched first," Dad said.

"But it wasn't Jonty," I insisted. "Bayard's been picking a fight with him for ages…"

"Tess," Dad said, in that firm voice he uses when he won't brook any argument. I stopped talking. "I didn't ask *you* what happened, I asked them. When I ask a question, I expect an answer. I've got no time or place for people who can't answer a simple question. So until they're ready to talk, they're off the job. Understand?"

"But…"

"No buts. Finish your lunch and we'll get back to work." He turned and walked back towards the woolshed. I started to follow him, then stopped. Bayard was in there, washing blood off his face with cold water, mopping it up with paper towels, while Jonty walked home down the dusty road, still bleeding. It wasn't fair, and I turned around and ran after him.

Jonty turned his head as I approached, his eyes dropping towards the ground the moment they met mine. I stopped next to him, breathing hard.

"Why did you fight him?"

Jonty looked offended. "He hit me first!"

"Oh so you were just defending yourself?"

"Tess. He punched me in the face, then pinned up against a wall and tried to hit me again. What was I supposed to do, just stand there and take it?"

I had no answer for that. The blood on his cheek had mostly dried, but a few bright red beads still sat on top of the cut. I dug into my pocket and pulled out a tissue, then dabbed at the wound.

"Why can't he just leave us alone?" I asked him sadly. "Why did he have to pick a fight?"

Jonty grabbed my wrist and slowly lowered my hand, then started walking again. I glared at his back for a moment, then called after him.

"Who was he with?"

Jonty stopped, looking back over his shoulder at me. "What?"

"You said you saw him at Hayley's party with someone," I insisted. "That's what started all this. So who was he with?"

Jonty looked alarmed. "You heard that?"

"I heard all of it," I told him. "I was there the whole time."

"Dammit." Jonty looked uncomfortable, averting his eyes and gazing over my shoulder. "I can't tell you that."

"What? Why not?" He just shook his head, and my anger bubbled. "Didn't you just threaten to tell *everyone*? Isn't that why he hit you? Come on, Jonty. I thought you trusted me."

He looked annoyed. "I do. But…look, I was never going to say anything. That was just a way to get him to stop talking about me. I didn't mean it."

"Why not?" I asked. "He started it."

"An eye for an eye makes the whole world blind," Jonty quoted. "It's not my secret to share, okay? Just leave it at that."

I just blinked at him for a long moment. I felt as though I was stuck holding the last piece of a jigsaw puzzle, staring at the space where I wanted it to fit, but it was completely the wrong shape. I rotated it in my head, trying to understand.

"But I don't get it. So he was with someone. So what?" I tried to remember who I'd seen him with at the party. "What could possibly be so bad about…" And then it fell into place, and changed the picture completely. "Wait. Was he with another guy?"

Jonty just kept walking, refusing to answer me.

"Jonty!"

"I told you that I'm not talking about it," he insisted. "Just leave it alone."

"God, you're infuriating," I snapped. "I feel like punching you myself right now."

Jonty stopped and faced me, then opened his arms wide, palms outward. "Give it your best shot."

"Oh stop being such a martyr," I told him irritably. "Go home and put some ice on that eye, and when you decide to stop being so bloody noble, you know where to find me."

"They weren't fighting over me, you know."

Dad turned his head away from the TV for a moment to consider me, then returned his attention to the screen.

"Didn't imagine that Bayard would bother. Seems like it'd be a lost cause."

I huffed out a breath. "Don't be too sure about that," I told him. "They're both idiots right now, if you ask me."

"Well, they're boys," Dad said. "Boys do stupid things. They'll probably grow out of it."

"I'm not going to hold my breath."

Dad looked slightly amused. The TV show he was watching went to an ad break, and he turned the sound off. The room was silent except for the gentle hum of the refrigerator.

"I went down to the cottage yesterday," he told me. "To take a look around."

I'd forgotten about his threat to evict Jonty's family. Despite how mad I was with Jonty just then, I knew that I didn't want him to leave. Jonty hadn't said anything, but he'd been in a touchy mood all day.

"What did you tell them?" I asked, my heart pounding.

"Nothing yet." He lifted a hand and scratched the stubble on his cheek that he'd let grow since Mum had been gone. "But it's falling down around them, Tess. I shouldn't have let them stay this long. It can't go on like this."

"But you can't kick them out!" I said. "Where will they go?"

Dad shook his head. "Honey, that's not my problem."

My jaw dropped. "So that's it, is it? You're just going to tell them to leave, and shrug it off and say it's not your problem if they starve?"

"Tess…"

"I thought you liked Jonty."

"I do."

"So don't do this. Please," I begged.

I couldn't get the image of little Phoebe dangling upside down from the tyre swing out of my head. They were happy there, had made it into as much of a home as possible in a place like that. It seemed cruel and unnecessary to send them away.

Dad sighed heavily. "Tess, my hands are tied. I can't let them go on living there. As a landlord, I'm responsible for that place and if anything goes wrong, it could cost us everything. We could lose the farm."

I scoffed. "Now you're just being dramatic."

"Am I? Do you have any idea how much debt we're in right now? We can't afford a lawsuit. And I'm not losing this place." He shook his head sadly. "Not for them."

I sat still for a moment, stunned. "Is it really that bad?"

Dad took a breath. "It's not good," he admitted. "Honey, I'm not a monster. You know that. I don't want to do this, but I don't see that I have a choice."

The show he was watching came back onscreen, and he turned the sound up. I sat in silence, my head spinning. My phone buzzed, and I checked the incoming message.

It was Katy, sending me a video of Misty jumping in her arena. He looked excited, but he jumped well and cleared everything. AJ had clearly done the filming, as I kept catching glimpses of Squib's ears at the bottom of the frame. Misty jumped the last fence and Katy cantered past the screen, smiling and patting him. The clip ended, frozen on that image, Katy leaning forward and patting his neck, Misty's back end lifting into the air as he threw in a casual buck.

"Will we have to sell the ponies?" I asked Dad.

He looked over at me, and shook his head. "I shouldn't have said anything. Don't worry, okay? We'll work things out." He held his arm out to me, and I moved in closer, snuggling against his shoulder. We'd grown closer in the past few days than we'd been in years.

"I'm glad you told me," I said, and he patted my shoulder.

I wondered how much Hayley's treatment was costing, and where that money was coming from. There had been a lot of times in my life that I'd wished I was older, more independent, that I was treated less like a child and more like an adult. But the older I got, the more I was starting to realise that adults didn't have all the answers. They were just better at pretending that they did. Maybe adulthood wasn't all it was cracked up to be, after all.

I couldn't imagine what Dad would do if we lost the farm. This place was his life, his passion. It was mine too. I'd always assumed that it would be in the family forever.

If we had to leave, I didn't know where else I'd go.

12

FIGURE IT OUT

We were up before daybreak the next morning to load the weaner calves onto the stock truck. They were uncertain, lost without the guidance of their mothers, and with only me, Hugh and Dad involved, it took us quite a while to get them up the high-sided stock ramp and onto the truck. They finally loaded, and Hugh went with the calves into Hastings to oversee the sale while Dad and I returned to the house for breakfast.

Neither Jonty nor Bayard had shown up for work. I'd heard Hugh muttering something to Dad about it, but they'd stopped talking when I came closer, and I knew I wasn't going to be privy to that conversation.

I fried bacon and eggs while Dad sipped black coffee and read the paper, turning straight to the Farming section as always. I put a plate of food down in front of him and sat down with my own breakfast.

"I did some research last night," I told Dad, who looked up at me in surprise. "And I have some questions for you."

"What about?"

"Do you charge the Fishers rent?"

Dad blinked at me. "Not officially. They paid us for a while, your mother insisted on it. But they started falling behind and were clearly struggling, so I let it go." He looked pained. "Feels a bit disingenuous now, considering the condition of the place."

"So if they're not paying rent, technically they're squatters," I continued. "Which means that you wouldn't be liable if anything went wrong, if they were there without your consent."

Dad's eyebrows shot up. "You want me to revoke my permission for them to be there?"

"Just technically," I said. "You only ever had a verbal agreement, right?" He nodded, much to my relief.

"What makes you think they'll agree to stay under those circumstances?" Dad asked. "Knowing that they're there illegally?"

"I don't," I admitted. "In fact, I think they're unlikely to. If they know." Dad frowned, and I clarified. "I think you should talk to Nate, and only Nate. He's not so…stubborn."

"You mean he has a weaker moral compass?" Dad suggested.

"Something like that."

Dad sighed. "I don't know, Tess. This could land all of us in a pile of hot water." I held my breath as he chewed on a large piece of bacon, then swallowed. "I don't know any of the legalities around it."

I was ready for that. "Aunty Helen's still a real estate agent, isn't she? Ring her up and ask her for advice. I'm sure she'd know, or could refer you to someone who does."

"You've been giving this a lot of thought, haven't you?" Dad asked. "Yes."

He reached for his coffee mug and had just picked it up when three things happened in quick succession. There was a knock at the door, Colin jumped up barking from where he'd been hiding under the table, and Dad sloshed hot coffee all over the newspaper.

"Bloody dog! Come in," he called in the same breath, and the door opened to reveal Bayard. I was disappointed – I'd hoped that Jonty would be the first to apologise. Bay looked nervous, lingering on the threshold. His nose was red and swollen, but I didn't feel too bad about it.

"Come in," Dad repeated. "And shut that mongrel outside, would you?" He looked at the sodden newspaper in exasperation as I ate the last of my bacon.

"You'd read it already," I told him as Bayard came slowly into the room.

"Not that part."

"Read it online?" I suggested, scraping egg yolk to the edge of my plate and licking it off my fork.

Dad didn't even dignify that suggestion with an answer, since he doesn't know how to use the computer, and turned his attention instead to Bayard.

"Well?"

Bayard spoke immediately. "I'm sorry. It won't happen again."

"Damn right it won't. I'm not having punch ups in the middle of the work day. You going to tell me what happened?"

Bay's face flushed red, and he looked at his boots before speaking, his voice almost inaudible. "I hit him." He swallowed hard, and spoke a little louder. "I hit him first."

"Did he provoke you?"

Bayard looked uneasy. "He...he said something. I overreacted."

"He wasn't going to tell anyone," I said, and Bayard's head snapped up to look at me. I met his eyes evenly.

"You...know?" he croaked out.

"Only because I guessed. I overheard your whole conversation, and I put two and two together." Bayard's face was bright red, and he wouldn't look at me. "Jonty wouldn't say anything, even after I figured it out. He said it wasn't his secret to tell."

Dad was looking from me to Bayard and back again with narrowed eyes. Colin started barking, and I sat up a little straighter. It was his happy, welcoming bark that he used for people he liked, and sure enough, moments later there were footsteps on the porch and another knock at the door.

"Go see who that is," Dad told me, even though we all knew who it would be. I got up and walked to the door, opening it to reveal Jonty. I wasn't surprised to see him, but his appearance shocked me. His cheek was swollen and his eye was purple and slightly bloodshot.

"Oh my God."

The corner of his mouth twitched in an attempt at a smile, but like Bayard before him, he looked nervous. "Is your Dad here?"

"Yeah, he's talking to Bayard right now."

"Oh." He hesitated, then stepped back. "Okay. I'll wait out here."

"You don't have to…"

But Dad had turned to look at him now. "Come in Jonty. Shut the door behind you."

Jonty willingly complied, and Dad raised his eyebrows at the sight of his face.

"You make a right pair, the two of you," he said, looking from Bayard's swollen nose to Jonty's black eye. "Jonty, what've you got to say for yourself?"

I expected him to follow Bayard's lead and immediately apologise to my father, but he didn't. Instead, he turned towards Bayard, speaking quickly.

"I never said anything to Tess, or anyone else. I swear. I know a thing or two about keeping secrets. You know that." Bay nodded without looking up and Jonty turned towards Dad. "I'm sorry for what happened yesterday. It was inappropriate, and it won't happen again."

Dad leaned back in his chair and considered them. "Well, that's two apologies. Now I have to decide what to do next." He looks from one to the other and back again. "You're both good workers. I don't want to lose either one of you. But I don't want to deal with this shit ever again. So either you can work together, or you can't."

Jonty spoke first. "I have no issue with Bayard, sir."

We all looked at Bayard, who was staring at his hands. He hesitated for a moment, then looked at Dad. "I can work with him."

Dad narrowed his eyes as my heart pounded. "You sure?"

Bayard nodded, glancing at Jonty, then back to Dad. "Yeah."

Dad pushed his chair back and stood up from the table. "Right. Both of you, get down to the yards and saddle up a horse each. I need the two-tooths brought down onto Plugge's before the end of the day. Bayard knows the way." Bay nodded as he stood up. "Jonty, get Hugh to put you on one of the farm hacks. It's almost eight now, I want you back by ten thirty at the latest."

"I'll come with you," I told Jonty as he made his way towards the door on Bayard's heels. "I was planning on going for an early ride anyway."

"No, Tess." Dad shook his head at me. "I want them out there on their own. They've got something to prove."

Jonty glanced over his shoulder and smiled at me. "See you when we get back."

Dad, Hugh and I were kept busy in the yards that morning, vaccinating the weaner calves that we'd decided to keep. Ted Petersen, an old friend of Dad's who had a farm down in Flemington, stopped in on his way to the weaner fair with his son-in-law Robbie, and they lent us a quick hand while I put the jug on and organised smoko for everyone.

As I poured boiling water over the teabags, I checked the time again. Ten twenty-five, and still no sign of Jonty or Bayard. I hoped that they were just delayed because the sheep were being difficult, not because they'd had an accident, or another falling-out. I carried the mugs of hot tea out to the yards, where Dad was standing with Ted and Robbie. A lit cigarette drooped from Ted's lower lip, sprinkling ash into his mug as he took it from my hands.

"Ta, love."

I handed Dad his cuppa and then turned to see two riders jogging across the paddock below us. Relief washed over me as I recognised the boys, and I leaned on the railing and watched them as they stopped to open a gate. Jonty manoeuvred the horse he was riding around to shut it behind them while Bayard's solid chestnut waited patiently. I rarely rode the farm hacks, and it took me a moment to recognise Jonty's plain bay gelding as Possum, the horse that Jock usually rode.

As the boys picked up an easy trot across the paddock, the difference in their riding abilities was evident, even from a distance. Bayard still sat like a sack of potatoes in the saddle, trusting more to Rusty's good nature than his own centre of gravity to keep him there, but Jonty rode as though he was a part of his horse. Even old Possum had a new spring in his step, and he was striding out happily across the dry grass.

One of the dogs started a rabbit and shot off in pursuit, but it disappeared into a hole before she could catch it. I recognised Midge, one of our most experienced working dogs who was flawless with sheep, but could be all too easily distracted by a rabbit, and often practiced selective deafness when she was called off them. True to form, she was shoving her muzzle into the rabbit hole as though willing herself to fit down it. Dad muttered something as Jonty stuck his fingers in his mouth and whistled. Midge's head shot up, and she turned to look at him. Jonty called her back, and miracle of miracles, she left the hole and came running back to him.

"Who is that?" Robbie asked curiously, leaning on the rails as he sipped his tea.

"Just a local boy we've been trialling," Dad said casually, but I could see that he was impressed with how well he had the dogs in hand.

"Sits well on a horse," Ted commented, taking another drag on his cigarette. "Bloody hard finding someone that can ride these days. They all want to be out on the quads, but there's plenty of places on ours that only a horse can take you. We're looking for another hand around the place, so if he doesn't work out for you, send him our way."

Dad glanced in my direction and raised an eyebrow. "You might have to ask this one's permission first."

I blushed as Ted grinned at me. "Ah, I see. Good for you, lass," he said, then turned to my father. "Always good when they find a decent farming bloke. Makes it a lot easier to hand a farm down to someone who knows what they're doing."

I saw a faint smile rise to Robbie's lips as he sipped his tea, and remembered that Ted didn't have any sons either. His daughter Rebecca had married Robbie a few years ago, and they already had two children. I leaned against the railing and watched Jonty, wondering what lay ahead for us. It didn't seem crazy to think of us staying on here, working on the farm alongside my parents, then taking it over when Dad retired. Mum would want me to go to university, but I could get an Agricultural Science degree, work out ways to make the farm more profitable and efficient so we could try to avoid getting into these slumps whenever the rain was late.

The future stretched out before me, endless in its possibilities. Hayley wanted to go to Europe and ride, it was all she'd talked about for years, although her plans had taken a backseat lately to her health. But she was on the mend now, had received a clean result after her MRI scan yesterday, and while she was still fragile, she was on the road to recovery. She could go and pursue her dreams, and I could stay here and live out mine.

Bayard said something to Jonty, making him throw his head back and laugh out loud. They were both grinning as they rode up to the gate into the yard paddock, apparently friends at last. I watched Jonty dismount smoothly, clapping Possum's neck and rubbing Midge's head before unlatching the gate and swinging it open. I looked at Ted's gnarled, work-worn hands resting on the railing next to mine and wondered if that would be Jonty in fifty years' time. There was nothing I wanted more than to be here, with him, across the years to come.

Tess! R U there?

I looked down at my phone and thumbed out a quick reply to Katy.

yep. Hows misty?

Dad made an irritated noise and I set my phone back down on the arm of the couch. He hated it when I texted while watching TV, and we'd sat down to this movie together. Even though I'd seen *Footrot Flats* close to a thousand times, Dad never got tired of it. I suppose it was the closest thing he had to a movie about his life. My phone buzzed again, and Dad frowned as I picked it back up.

Hes insane! but in a good way haha. U coming to HOY?

I looked at Dad, who turned his head slightly towards me, one eye still fixed on the screen. "What?"

"The Horse of the Year Show starts on Tuesday," I told him.

He nodded. "I'm aware."

"Can I go?" He picked up the remote control and hit pause, then turned to face me. "Katy's asking. And I want to go and watch Misty. I think one of us should."

"Hmm." Dad scratched the back of his head. "When's he jumping?"

"Thursday through Sunday."

Mum had sent in the entry weeks ago when I'd still been planning to ride. Misty had a 1.20m warm-up class on Thursday, the 1.25m Championship Stakes on Friday, Pony of the Year on Saturday, and, depending on how that went, the Speed Pony of the Year on Sunday. Katy had swapped our entries into her name, but the schedule was unchanged.

"You want to take two days off school for a show you're not riding at?"

"One day," I corrected him. "Friday's a teacher only day this week, so it would only be Thursday. I could stay in Katy's truck. Probably," I amended. Katy's truck was pretty limited for accommodation, and she'd already have AJ and her mum with her. I wondered briefly about Susannah's truck, which was huge, but I wasn't sure about asking her, and I found her overbearing father intimidating. "Or you could drive our truck up and we could stay in that, then bring Misty home after the show finishes."

Dad leaned back against the cushions, thinking. "You don't want to leave him with Katy for the winter?"

The thought hadn't even crossed my mind. "No, I think Hayley will want him to be here."

"It's going to be a while before she can ride again," Dad reminded me. "And you're the one who said Misty shouldn't be going to waste in the paddock."

"Jonty will ride him," I said. "He won't mind, and Misty likes him. Trust me, Dad. Hayley will want Misty to be here when she gets back."

He gave in. "All right, fine. I'll drop you up there in the truck on Thursday."

I grinned and hugged him around his broad shoulders. "Thank you!"

"Yeah, yeah. I just want you out of my hair," he teased.

"Yeah right. You'll be lost without me and you know it. But don't worry, I'll make you a lasagne and a casserole before I go. That should keep you going."

Dad smiled. "I'm sure I'll be fine, but thanks." He lifted the remote and restarted the movie, then paused it again a second later. "Hang on. What's this about *we could stay in the truck*? Who is *we*, exactly?" I felt my face flush, and he shook his head adamantly. "No."

"Please?"

"No. Absolutely not, Tess. You know I like Jonty, but I'm not

156

sending you up to HOY to spend two nights alone in a truck with him. Out of the question."

"You can trust us," I insisted. "I promise." But I could tell he wouldn't be swayed, so I quickly brainstormed other options. "What if we bring the pup tent, and he sleeps in that?"

Dad looked unconvinced. "And you'll sleep in the truck on your own?"

"Or AJ could stay with me, instead of being stuck sleeping in Katy's cab. She'd love it." I knew what Dad was thinking, and did my best to reassure him that there would be no loss of virtue on my part. "Katy's mum will be there to supervise and make sure we, uh, stick to our word." Dad raised an eyebrow and I felt my cheeks flush as we danced around that topic. "I'll get her to ring you now, if you want, so you can discuss it."

"Is it really that important to you?" he asked.

"Yes."

"Why?"

I bit my lip, wondering how to explain. "Because…" *Because I love him* wasn't going to cut it. I was almost sixteen, but Dad still saw me as a child, and I knew he wasn't ready for that declaration. I wasn't entirely sure that I was either. "Because I don't get lonely when I'm with him. Because he knows what these last few months have been like, and he notices when I'm upset, even when I'm trying to hide it. And he takes care of me, and I know I'm supposed to be a strong confident young woman but I need that right now. Because I don't know how I would've got through all this without him."

Dad drummed his fingers against the bottom of the remote, and I knew he was considering my proposition.

"Sounds like he's pretty important to you."

"You know he is."

Dad sighed, and I knew he would concede. "All right then. *If* Katy's mum agrees."

"Thanks Dad! I'll get her to ring you right now," I said, hastily texting Katy back as Dad resumed watching his movie. Halfway through composing my message, I paused and looked at my father. "I'm glad you like Jonty."

Dad shrugged. "Well, he's all right. Works hard, does as he's told. Hardly ever gets into fights." I laughed, but only a flicker of a smile crossed Dad's face. "He'll do."

I couldn't help asking. "For what?"

Dad glanced at me with narrowed eyes. "For now."

The Horse of the Year Show is one of the busiest weekends on the Hawke's Bay calendar, bringing people from all across New Zealand into Hastings and its surrounding towns and villages. Hotels and campsites are booked out months in advance by spectators and retailers, while almost all of the competitors camp onsite in their trucks, floats and occasionally tents alongside their horses and ponies. Temporary yards pop up all over the place, lining the boundary fences all the way around the grounds, and the covered yards and stables are packed to capacity. Each year the show gets bigger, and there's always a precarious balance between the cost of running the event and the tourism benefits that it brings to the area.

"You made it!"

AJ came bounding across the grass towards our truck as we drove in, dressed in her summer horse show uniform of shorts, paddock boots and a singlet top covered in hay, horse hair and slobber marks. A layer of dirt covered her from head to toe as the Hawke's Bay sun was out in full force and the recent drought conditions had baked the ground dry. Thousands of hooves had now stirred up the dust, covering horse and human alike. I climbed down from the cab and she threw her arms around me as soon as my feet hit the grass, squeezing me tight. She'd definitely made a full recovery from that broken collarbone, because her hug was as bone-crunching as ever.

"Talked Mum into it somehow," I grinned.

Actually, Mum had readily agreed to the plan, probably relieved that I hadn't renounced show jumping entirely, although she hadn't been so thrilled about Jonty accompanying me, and it had taken another, much longer phone call to Katy's mum to convince her that I was going to come home with my virtue intact, so to speak.

"You can park in there," she told us, pointing to a narrow space between Katy's truck and the chain link fence that bordered the car park. "It'll be a bit of a squeeze, but we figured you only had to get yourselves – I mean, ourselves," she edited with a wink, "in and out, and not worry about ponies and tack and stuff. So we thought that'd be enough room, and believe you me, we've had enough trouble trying to stop people from parking there already, including one enormous polo truck that took like ten horses. No idea how they thought they would fit, but they seemed determined."

"Thanks for chasing them off," I told her.

"Oh, that was Katy, not me. She's surprisingly fierce when she wants to be," AJ laughed as Katy appeared.

She was still wearing her riding clothes, a hot pink sleeveless shirt and breeches that had probably been white this morning, but were now closer to tan.

"Hey, you mess with the bull," Katy said, giving me a quick hug that was only slightly less bone-crunching than AJ's had been. "They tried to park there after dark, the idiots, so after that we just set up a tent there and left a small light on inside it all night so people could see it and would be too scared to park there in case they flattened someone's family member."

I laughed. "Good job. How's Misty?"

"He's fine. Excited, right up on his toes and he can't wait to jump tomorrow," she grinned. "How's Hayley?"

"Doing well, apparently," I told them. "She's still in Auckland, so I haven't seen her, but Mum said she's on the right track."

"Awesome. I'm so glad."

"Yeah, me too."

Jonty had jumped down from the cab and was directing Dad as he backed carefully into the narrow space. Mum usually drove the truck, and while Dad was a good driver used to handling various farm machinery, the truck was bigger than his tractor and much less forgiving of being backed into something.

"I'm so glad you're here," AJ said. "This is going to be awesome. Susannah's parked next to Katy, but I think she's still out competing. The metre-fifteen has been running for literally hours already. If they don't get their act together, they'll have people jumping in the dark like they did last year."

"And not under lights, like at proper shows," Katy added with a roll of her eyes. "Literally in the dark, until they had to cancel it for safety's sake. I had Forbes in one of those rounds and he almost killed me."

Dad looked relieved as he parked the truck and climbed down, wiping sweat off his brow. "Bloody unwieldy thing," he muttered.

"Hey, at least it's got power steering," I told him. "The first truck you bought us didn't, and Mum was forever bumping into things and getting stuck."

"Thanks Tess, I do remember," he said, coming over to us and saying a quick hello to my friends. "Right, you sorted?" I nodded, and he held out the truck keys, dropping them into my palm. "*Don't* lose them."

"Promise."

"Okay."

He gave me a hug, told me to behave myself, said goodbye to Jonty and walked towards the gate, where Hugh was going to meet him with the ute and give him a ride back home.

AJ and Katy almost immediately fell into an argument about whether we should go and see if Susannah had jumped yet, or whether mucking out Katy's yards and feeding her ponies took priority. By the time we'd collectively decided to go and watch Forbes jump now then all pitch in and do the mucking out later, Susannah had appeared.

"Did we miss it?" AJ demanded. "We were just coming to watch!"

Susannah pulled a face and dismounted. "I'm glad you didn't. it was horrible. Hi Tess, hi Jonty," she added as she ran up Forbes' stirrups.

"What'd he do?" Katy asked as the four of us followed Susannah curiously back to her truck.

She tied Forbes to the ring on the side of it and unbuckled his girth. "Usual shenanigans. Napped at the gate going in, threatened to refuse at every jump that had fill in it, and took three rails. On the bright side, he didn't rear, so…" She shrugged as she pulled the saddle off his sweaty back. "He was just fed up. The class is running so late, and someone fell off when I was three away and it took her about ten minutes to decide to stand up and walk out of the ring."

"Ugh, I hate when people lie there like they're dying for hours and then just get up and walk off," Katy grumbled uncharitably. "Like you're either fine or you're not, and you know that when you hit the ground, so don't flail around down there wasting everyone's time."

"You're both horrible people and I'm ashamed to know you," AJ said breezily, rolling her eyes at me. "I hope you both fall off tomorrow and learn a valuable lesson about empathy."

"Thanks best friend, it's nice to know I can always count on your support," Katy replied.

"Anytime," AJ assured her. "Come on then, let's go get those yards mucked out like you were so desperate to do a few minutes ago."

We left Susannah to untack Forbes and walked over to the yards to see Misty, Molly and Puppet. Misty's head was buried past his eyeballs inside his hay bag, snuffling out every last piece of hay.

"He's such an egg," I said, smiling at him. "Misty, you weirdo.

What're you doing?"

At the sound of my voice, he lifted his head. The hay bag was caught on his halter, and it stayed over his muzzle, muffling his welcoming whinny. He shook his head firmly, the hay bag fell away and he paced to the corner of his yard and stared at me as though he could hardly believe I was there.

"Aw, he's missed you!" AJ beamed.

"Apparently," I replied. "He's never looked pleased to see me before in his life. Funny he should start now."

"Not really," AJ said. "He probably thought you sold him or something."

I reached Misty's yard and ducked under the railing. He bunted me hard with his head, then proceeded to search me thoroughly for apples or carrots. It didn't take him long to sniff out the peppermints in my pocket, and I fished a couple out for him. He snatched them off my palm with a sharp nip that made me wince.

"You bully," I told him, looking at the blood blister that was forming. "You ever hear about not biting the hand that feeds you?"

Misty was typically unfazed by my scolding, pushing past me to greet Jonty at the gate and molest him for treats as well.

"Get out of it," Jonty told him affectionately, pushing him backwards as he brought the muck fork and skip bucket in. "I see your manners haven't improved while you've been away."

Despite his antics, Misty genuinely seemed pleased to see us. He chewed at my hair while I struggled to untie the hay bag that Katy had secured to the rail with about ten thousand knots, and I had to offer him another peppermint to convince him to let go of my ponytail once I was done.

"Demon child," I told him fondly as Jonty and I exited his yard.

Misty batted his eyelashes at me and I rubbed his broad forehead before following AJ back to the truck to fetch another bale of hay.

13

FRACTURE

"I actually can't believe your parents are allowing this," Katy said incredulously as Jonty dealt another hand of cards.

It was almost ten o'clock and pitch dark outside, but the five of us were still wide awake, sitting in our truck after demolishing several pizzas and about a dozen cans of Coke between us.

"Allowing what?" I asked, and Katy arched an eyebrow at me, her meaning clear.

"Get your mind out of the gutter Kathryn," Jonty told her, flipping a card onto the pile in front of her. "AJ's sleeping in here tonight, remember?"

"Yeah, and you're sleeping in the tent alone," Katy said sarcastically. "*Sure.*"

"He'd better be," AJ retorted. "I don't want to be woken up in the middle of the night by any hanky panky."

Susannah snorted, then winced as Coca-Cola bubbles went up her nose. She swallowed, her eyes watering. "Hanky panky?"

"What would you call it?"

"Not that," she shrugged.

"Well I hope you packed earplugs," Katy told AJ, scooping up the cards that Jonty had finished dealing. "Because I don't rate your chances."

"Hey," Jonty said. "I do have some honour, you know."

"Sure. That's what they all say," Katy replied.

"Give him some credit," AJ argued. "He's kept his hands off Tess for almost the past hour. That's got to be some kind of new record."

"Have I really?" Jonty asked. "Better start playing catch-up then." And he wrapped his arms around my waist and pulled me in towards him, nuzzling my neck.

"Okay stop, I'll go blind," Katy said, shielding her eyes with her hand.

Jonty let me go and reached for his can of Coke. "Her parents make the rules; I just follow them."

"I'm not sure what's crazier, that they made those rules or that they actually expect you to stick to them," Katy replied.

AJ rolled her eyes. "I know this is news to you, Katy, but some people actually do as they're told. Shocking, I know."

Katy kicked her in the shin, and AJ wasted no time dealing a retaliatory punch to Katy's arm.

"Ow!"

"Shouldn't have kicked me," AJ said with a shrug, picking up the hand that Jonty had just dealt her and pulling a face. "Seriously? Okay, that's the last time we let Jonty deal."

"Seconded," Susannah said, eyeing her own hand with equal disgust.

I picked up my cards and fanned them out, revealing a very good hand.

"Never play poker, Tess," AJ told me, watching the expression on my face. "I feel like I should just throw my hand in now, but what can I say? I'm a sucker for punishment." She leaned back against the cushions and elbowed Katy in the side. "Hurry up woman, you have to give Tess your top two cards before we start."

The truck's side door swung open as Katy rearranged her hand, and Deb poked her head inside.

"Katy, time for bed."

Her daughter pulled a face at her. "What am I, five?"

"Well, sometimes I wonder," Deb replied. "Come on, you've got big classes tomorrow."

"After we've played this hand," Katy said dismissively.

I expected Deb to double down, but she sighed and retreated. AJ rolled her eyes at me as Katy plucked two cards from her hand and slid them across the table to me, taking the two I'd offered her with a grimace.

"This game sucks."

"Nobody's making you play," Jonty told her, leading with a pair of threes. "You could do as you're told and go to bed."

"What is this, gang up on Katy day?"

"Oh stop moaning and start playing," AJ told her.

Katy stuck her tongue out at her friend, looked at her hand and sighed. "Pass."

AJ beat Jonty's threes with a pair of aces, making everyone groan as another knock came on the door. This time it was Susannah's father, also there to tell his daughter to go to bed. Unlike Katy, Susannah threw in her hand immediately.

"Be right there," she told him, and he left as she started picking up her things. "Where's my phone?"

"On the bench," I told her and she grabbed it.

"Okay. Night, guys."

"Are you really leaving? Finish this hand," Katy complained, but Susannah shook her head.

"Dad's been really good so far this week," she said. "I can't afford to piss him off." She pushed the door open. "It's the price I pay for my independence."

We called goodnight to her as she left, shutting the door behind her.

"She's such a goody-good," Katy grumbled. "Pass."

I won the hand, cleared the table and led with triple queens.

"Right, I give up," AJ declared, throwing her cards face up onto the table to reveal a very weak hand. "Susannah's gone, Tess is slaying and I'm pretty sure that Jonty's got both the Jokers, so it's hardly worth sticking around to be annihilated."

We were up by six the next morning, and the day passed in a haze of sunshine, junk food and hard work. Ponies were fed and mucked out and taken for a morning leg stretch, then the grooming began, washing legs and tails, brushing them until they glistened. Running back and forward from the rings to the truck, keeping an eye on the order of go, watching Katy and Susannah trot around the dusty warm-up, adjusting the practice fences for them, standing beside the ring and crossing our fingers as they jumped, hoping for a good outcome. Leading Misty back and forth, dodging his playful nips until Katy was ready for him, her face already filmed with dust from her clear round on Molly. Misty's short legs pistoning across the ground, his knees tucked tight through the air, an unfortunate rail at the last keeping them out of the jump off. Hosing the sweat off his broad back, poulticing and wrapping his legs and taking him for a walk and a pick of grass before refilling his hay bag. Eating hot chips and icecream for lunch while we watched the Seven Year Old Final from the grandstand, going shopping with Susannah's dad's credit card and encouraging her to buy all the things we wished we could afford, eating icecream and ogling the cross-country jumps scattered throughout the grounds, ready for the eventing on Saturday afternoon. Heading back to the yards and getting Puppet ready for his class, watching him jump double clear and finish a very close second in the 1.10m Final, cheering Katy on her lap of honour around the Premier Arena. Walking over to the polo grounds in the late afternoon, sitting under the trees and watching Susannah school Forbes in smooth circles on the green grass while Jonty lay on his back and dozed with his hands behind his head. Back to the yards again, pausing to watch an exciting jump off in the NRM Arena then mucking out again, filling up hay nets, making feeds and walking the ponies out to stretch their legs. Sitting on the crushed grass in the car park while the ponies picked at it as locals and tourists slowly drove out, heading back home or to their hotels for the night, then putting the ponies away, walking back to the trucks for dinner, tack cleaning and, eventually, several more rounds of cards.

The five of us quickly became a team, all pitching in to help each other and take care of the ponies. Although both Katy's mum and Susannah's dad were around, the bulk of the horse care was left to us. It was the most fun I'd ever had at a show, and I collapsed into bed that evening thoroughly exhausted.

"Ready, Misty?"

The grey pony bunted me with his head, and I patted his solid neck as the gate steward nodded Katy into the Premier Arena. It was the first round of the Pony Championship Stakes, the final warm-up round for most before the Pony of the Year tomorrow afternoon. I stepped out of the way as Katy shortened her reins and Misty shot forward, bounding exuberantly into the arena. We crowded through the gate and stood in a huddle, watching as the previous rider took all three top rails off the treble, then tried to gallop down to the final oxer and ended up with a sliding refusal.

The hooter sounded to stop the rider so the fence could be rebuilt, and I saw Misty go into a half-rear, then plunge forward, making spectators along the fence line shrink backwards in alarm.

"He thought that was his starter," I said, my heart thumping.

Katy was struggling to circle the over-excited pony, and she looked over at me in some alarm.

"Any advice?" she asked as Misty skittered sideways, resisting her attempts to circle him.

"Hold on tight?" I suggested, and she grinned.

"I'll try. Misty, settle down you egg, that wasn't meant for you."

"Take him for a trot around, keep him moving," Deb told her daughter, and before I could contradict her, Katy had headed off down the long side.

"Not sure that was the right idea," Jonty said, echoing my own thoughts as Misty spooked at a trade tent and almost flattened one of the pole pickers, who had to leap out of his way. "Best just to keep him in one spot and keep him focused."

"You could've said so," Deb muttered, but Katy seemed to have worked out for herself that she was going the wrong way about this, and had moved Misty into the middle of the ring and was trotting him in a circle when the hooter went again to restart the previous rider.

This time Misty went into a full-height rear, and Katy flung her arms around his neck as he went up. A few people in the crowd gasped, and as Misty touched down, I realised that I'd grabbed Jonty's hand and was squeezing it tight.

"Sit up," I muttered as Misty shot forward and started trying to buck Katy off in retaliation for what he seemed to think was her refusal to let him at the jumps when he was supposed to have started already.

Fortunately for her, the pony that was competing cantered right past them, and Misty's attention was captured. I don't think he'd realised there was another pony in the ring, and he stood still and watched with pricked ears as the striking black gelding made a second attempt at the final oxer. His rider galloped towards it and I cringed as they got there flat and deep, but the pony had heart and scraped over, leaving the rails up and heading through the flags.

"An unfortunate eighteen faults there for Morag Friedman and HK Centurion," the announcer said. "In the ring now we have Misty Magic, ridden by Katy O'Reilly, and he looks like he's raring to go."

The hooter sounded for the third time, and Katy closed her legs around Misty's side. Misty threw in a ferocious buck, almost unseating her, then started bounding towards the first jump. Katy scrambled to get her stirrups back, recovering them just in time as Misty launched himself into the air over the first fence, clearing it by almost a foot.

"He's jumping like your pony," Jonty told AJ, who laughed.

"Squib's a lot better behaved than that, thank you," she retorted as Misty charged down to the second fence, fighting Katy on every stride, then flung himself over that one with equal abandon.

I had my heart in my mouth as I watched Misty continue around the course. He landed off fence four and bucked the whole way around the corner with his head tucked into his chest. Katy managed to get his head up a couple of strides out, sat down hard and kicked him on. Misty jumped high, landed short and added a half stride on his way to the oxer, which he had to really stretch out to clear. He made it, but with his ears flattened back against his head.

"Man, she's got him wired," Jonty said quietly.

"He's always like that," I said, but Susannah disagreed.

"Not with you he isn't." I stared at her, but she was insistent. "What? Tell me I'm wrong," she challenged Jonty and AJ.

"She's right," AJ said. "He's way calmer with you."

"He doesn't feel like it," I said honestly as Misty plunged around the corner, hauling at the reins. "He feels like that."

"Well he doesn't look it," Susannah assured me. "I know he went like that with Hayley too, but he always seemed a lot happier with you on him." I stared at her, and she shrugged. "Just my opinion. I could be wrong."

"You're not," AJ said. "It's Katy's hot seat that riles him up. Squib hates her too."

"Yeah, we noticed," Jonty said, remembering when Katy had briefly shown Squib with disastrous results.

"Um, guys. Isn't Katy supposed to be our friend?" I reminded them.

"Don't worry, she knows," AJ assured me. "Well, she knows she can't ride Squib, at least. To be perfectly honest with you, I think she knows she can't ride Misty that well either, but she's psychologically unable to admit defeat. Also she's worried that she'll get given something in Ireland to ride that goes like that, and she'll make a fool of herself if she can't get it done."

"She's clear so far," I pointed out in Katy's defence.

As I spoke, Katy saw a long distance two strides out from an oxer and kicked on to it. Misty shot forward, overreacting to her driving aid and caught the front pole on his way up. It clattered to the ground behind them, and I held my breath as Misty fired off a series of retaliatory bucks. He hated taking rails, especially when he deemed it to be the rider's fault for putting him in a bad spot. I knew the feeling well.

"Commentator's curse!" AJ declared, blaming me.

"And now he's mad," Jonty said as Misty came down to the treble. "This could get messy if she misses her stride going in."

But Katy was far too accomplished for that. She'd learned from her mistake, and steadied Misty up on the approach. They jumped cleanly through the combination, powered down to the final oxer and leapt over that one as well.

"Just the four faults for Misty Magic, but that won't be good enough to get them through to the jump off this time," the announcer said Katy trotted Misty towards the gate.

I felt a wave of disappointment for her, but Katy looked nonplussed.

"Oh well, she's got Molly through to the jump off already," AJ reminded me as Susannah ran off to get Skip warmed up, and we met Katy at the gate.

"Man he was strong!" she exclaimed, struggling to hold Misty back to a walk as he charged under the archway, foaming heavily at the mouth. "I thought he was going to go straight through some of those fences!"

"So did we," AJ said frankly. "You can probably take the spurs off, you know. Just a suggestion."

"You can probably bite me," Katy replied. "Just a suggestion."

Jonty and I looked at each other as they walked down the chute towards the warm-up, still bickering, and he grinned.

"Your friends are weird."

"I know."

We followed Katy back to where her mum was waiting with Molly. Katy jumped down and turned her attention to her own pony as AJ ran up Misty's stirrups and loosened his girth.

"Hi Tess."

I turned to see Anna Harcourt, leaning against the barrier with her dark grey show jacket casually slung over one arm.

"Oh hi Anna. How're you?"

She pulled a face. "I've been better. Saxon's been going like crap all week. I don't know what's wrong with him but he better get his act together before Pony of the Year tomorrow."

I grimaced sympathetically, watching Misty out of the corner of my eye as he dragged AJ towards the showing area.

"I'm sure he'll be fine," I said blandly, then looked at Jonty. "Where's she going?"

"Dunno. Want me to go help her?"

I watched AJ brace one foot against the ground and pull Misty's head around, then lead him back towards us. "No, I think she's got it."

"I see Misty's up to his usual tricks," Anna said, following my line of sight. "The number of times I've seen him dragging Hayley past our truck…" She looked at me guiltily. "How is she, by the way?"

"She's doing okay," I reassured Anna. "Surgery went well, and she's on track with her recovery."

Anna looked genuinely relieved. "That's great! Is she coming to watch tomorrow?"

"Uh, no. She's still in Auckland," I explained, my attention once again diverted by Misty, who was twirling in a circle around AJ while she attempted to hold him still. "I'd better go. Good luck tomorrow."

"Thanks. I'll need it! Tell Hayley I said hi!" she called after me.

"I will," I promised, then hurried over to AJ. "D'you want me to take him?"

"Absolutely," she said, handing his reins over willingly. "Tag, you're it."

"Come on monster," I told Misty, leading him away. "Let's get you cooled off."

Jonty stayed to watch Katy's jump off while I took Misty back to the truck and unsaddled him, then walked him down to the hosing bay. He stood happily under the stream of water without even fidgeting, which was a breakthrough for him, since he usually violently objected to being clean.

"Are you feeling okay?" I asked Misty as I led him, dripping, back to the truck. "You're being so good. It's weird."

Misty shunted me with his nose, making me stumble forward and almost fall flat on my face. A hand grabbed my arm, helping me recover my balance.

"Careful! You okay?"

I looked up to see Connor Campbell grinning at me, and I nodded, blushing.

"Fine, thanks." I kept walking, my face on fire, then turned to eyeball Misty. "Point taken. You're still a jerk."

I was wrapping Misty's legs with ice boots when I heard AJ's voice and looked up. She was leading Molly, with Jonty on the other side of her, and Susannah riding along behind them. Skip had a wide yellow sash around his neck, and I smiled at Susannah as I stood up, wiping my hands on my shorts.

"Well done!"

"Thanks," she said quietly before jumping off Skip's back and taking him to her truck.

I looked at the other two, suddenly realising that one of us was missing.

"Where's Katy?"

AJ and Jonty glanced at each other, both looking unusually serious.

"Ambulance," Jonty told me as AJ tied Molly up to the truck and started untacking her.

"Oh my God! Is she okay? What happened?"

"Yeah, she's fine. Well, they think she's broken her wrist, but she's okay otherwise," he said. "Molly stopped in the double, and Katy took a flier."

"You witch," AJ told the pony as she pulled the saddle off her hot back. "What's your excuse for that kind of behaviour?"

"Maybe she got sick of being the well-behaved one," Jonty suggested.

AJ scoffed. "You clearly haven't met Molly before. Well-behaved is a misnomer."

"Hey, look on the bright side," Jonty said. "At least it didn't happen in Pony of the Year."

"Won't get a chance to now," AJ said. "It starts in less than twenty-four hours, and even Katy can't ride with a freshly-broken wrist. You just wasted your chance to be a champion," she told Molly. "I hope you're proud of yourself."

Molly shook her head as AJ removed the bridle, seeming unfazed by the turn of events.

"Why don't you ride her instead?" Jonty suggested, and AJ laughed.

"No way. Katy can't ride Squib, and I can't ride Molly. Trust me, I've tried. She'd just throw me into the first jump and be done with it. No thank you." She pushed Molly away as the pony tried to rub her head on AJ's shoulder. "But if you still want Misty ridden, Susannah might do it."

I stared at her in surprise, the thought never having crossed my mind. "I…I don't know. D'you think she would?"

"Sure. Why not? You should ask her."

"Maybe," I said. "I'll think about it."

"You make a decision yet about Misty?"

I shook my head at Jonty, then took another sip of soda. I really had to stop drinking the stuff, because all the sugar was making my skin break out, but I couldn't help it. At the end of a long hot dusty day, I'd had about as much water as I could stomach. I stretched my legs out in front of me and crossed them over at the ankles, finally clean after my shower. Katy was still at the hospital having her cast on, but the rest of us had sorted the ponies out. AJ and Susannah were at the showers, and I was taking the opportunity to spend some quiet time alone with Jonty.

"Why don't you ride him?"

I spluttered, spitting Coke back into the can before wiping my mouth with the back of my hand. "What?"

"I'm serious. Why not?"

"Um, let me think. Because I can't."

"Why not?"

"Jonty, stop it. You know why."

He shrugged, shoving another handful of chips into his mouth.

"Besides, if you're so keen for him to compete, then why don't *you*?"

"Can't," he reminded me. "I'm not registered."

"We could sign you up for a day registration," I offered. "That's a thing, right?"

"Dunno. I don't think it'd work at HOY though. And besides, I've got nothing to wear. You, on the other hand," he said, getting to his feet and pulling open the door to the narrow wardrobe, "have plenty of options."

"How about *Because I don't want to*?" I asked him. "Is that a good enough excuse?"

"Not really."

Frustrated tears pricked the corners of my eyes. "Stop it," I begged him. "Please."

Jonty sighed and came back over to sit down next to me. "Tess, you know I wouldn't tell you to do something you couldn't do. But it's not that you can't." He put his arm across my shoulders and looked me in the eye. "It's that you're afraid to try. And it's okay to be afraid, that's normal. Everyone gets scared sometimes. But not trying is just… It's like you're giving up on yourself. And I hate seeing you do that."

"When do I do that?"

He raised an eyebrow. "When don't you?"

I pulled away from him, getting to my feet. "Well shit, Jonty. If I'm that much of a disappointment, maybe you should just go home and leave me to wallow in it."

He looked alarmed. "I didn't mean…don't get upset."

"Don't get upset? You tell me that I'm pathetic and a quitter, then tell me not to be upset?"

"I never said that. You're putting words in my mouth."

"It's what you meant," I insisted. "*Just try, Tess.* As if I haven't been trying, as if that's been my problem all along. Oh, if I just decided to *try*, then I wouldn't be scared anymore. Why didn't I think of that? Oh right, because it's bullshit!"

"If you say so," Jonty said, getting to his feet as the door swung open to reveal AJ and Susannah.

"We're starving, are you guys ready for dinner?" AJ asked cheerfully. She looked from me to Jonty, and frowned. "Is everything okay?"

"Fine. I'm going to check on Misty," I said, pushing past her and Susannah and storming over to the yards.

I could hear Jonty talking to them as I walked away, probably telling his side of the story and making himself sound reasonable instead of insane. Someone called out my name as I passed their truck, but I ignored them. I wasn't in the mood to talk to anyone right now.

Misty looked surprised to see me, and was clearly disappointed that I hadn't brought him any treats.

"Not even a peppermint," I confessed to him.

He huffed in disgust and went back to his hay, and I leaned on the railing and watched him eat, trying to calm my temper. I hardly ever flared up like that – it was far more Hayley's style than mine – but I hadn't been able to help myself. Having the one person who'd always seemed to understand, who'd always been on my side, turn around and tell me that I was just being stupid for being scared was like a stab in the heart.

I dropped my head and stared at the ground, trying not to cry because there were still people around and I didn't need anyone to ask me what was wrong, although they'd probably think that they already knew.

"Hey."

I turned my head to see Susannah standing awkwardly next to me. I sniffed, and wiped my eyes.

"Hi. I'm fine."

"Sure. You look great."

I managed to laugh. "Thanks." We stood in silence for a moment, but I had to ask. "Did you want something?"

"I just came to say that if you want me to ride Misty for you tomorrow, and I mean really want me to, not just asking me because you feel like you're obliged as a friend or anything, then I will. Well, I'll try anyway. I can't guarantee it'll go well."

I looked at Misty, my thoughts whirling around in my head.

"Um…"

"Only if you want me to. I really don't care either way. I just thought I'd offer." Susannah spoke quickly, tripping over her words in her haste to reassure me.

"It's not that I don't think you could ride him," I told her honestly. "It's…well, I just don't know how Hayley would feel about it."

"I get it."

"Sorry."

"No, really. Don't be. Besides, I'm sure it doesn't matter to Misty whether he jumps or not."

I nodded, looking at Misty as he savagely pulled ripped hay from his hay bag. "True."

Susannah stepped back from the rail, still holding it with one hand. "Dinner's ready, by the way."

"Thanks. I'll be there soon."

"Okay," she said, and walked away.

I looked at Misty, who was watching her go as he chewed his hay. "What do you want to do, Misty? Stand in a yard all day tomorrow, or jump in Pony of the Year?"

It was a coincidence, of course, that Misty pricked up his ears and looked at me with interest when I said those last words. It didn't mean anything, wasn't a sign from the universe or a nudge from fate. It was just a coincidence, and I turned and walked back to the truck, trying to convince myself of that.

14

FORTUNE FAVOURS THE BRAVE

There was a heavy dew lying across the grounds the next morning. I got up early to feed and muck out Misty, but still wasn't early enough to beat Jonty to the job. He was in Misty's yard, nudging him over with his elbow while Misty laid his ears back and whisked his tail irritably at Jonty.

"You need to get yourself some manners," Jonty told him.

Misty wrinkled his nostrils in response, then saw me and hurried to the rail, his argument with Jonty forgotten. I leaned over and patted him, then gave him the apple he'd seen in my hand.

Jonty straightened up and saw me. "Morning."

"Hi," I said shyly.

Things had still been awkward between us last night after our fight, and we'd gone to bed early without really resolving anything. Jonty flipped the forkload of manure into the wheelbarrow and leaned on the railing next to me.

"I'm sorry."

"Me too. I shouldn't have shouted at you."

He shrugged. "I probably deserved it. I just…" He shook his head, and closed his mouth.

"What?"

"Doesn't matter."

"Go on, spit it out."

He smiled as he shook his head. "Nah. I'm learning to keep my mouth shut. It's taken a few years, but I think I'm getting the hang of it."

I could tell from the look on his face that he was committed to silence. He had the same look in his eye that he'd had when he'd refused to tell me about Bayard, and I knew how stubborn he could be. Misty lipped at my ponytail, then took a large hunk of it between his teeth and started pulling on it.

"Oi! Misty, cut it out!" I cried as Jonty came to my rescue, successfully distracting Misty with a peppermint out of his pocket. "Just when I was starting to like you," I told the pony ruefully, rubbing my stinging scalp.

"He's bored," Jonty said. "Needs to get out and stretch his legs." He looked at me sideways, then back at Misty. "I can take him for a ride, if you want."

I drew in a breath, then let it out. "I'll do it."

Jonty looked surprised. "Really?"

"Yeah. It's about time I got back on him."

"You don't have to."

"I know," I said, smiling despite the anxiety bubbling frantically within me. "That's why I want to."

Misty was a bundle of barely-contained energy, fizzing beneath me as I rode him across the road to the polo field. There were dressage arenas set up, the low white railings shining brightly in the sun, and horses and ponies trotting in every direction. Misty got up onto his toes, his ears pricked sharply forward, and I took a deep breath in, then let it slowly out. Jonty, walking alongside us, reached up and patted Misty's cresty neck reassuringly.

"Give him a job to do," he told me. "Get his attention somehow."

That was easier said than done, but I made an effort. Misty was like a pot that was about to boil over, and I shortened my reins and touched him lightly with my leg, signalling him to trot on. He burst forward into a canter, chucking at the bit, and a wave of panic swept over me. But it was followed just seconds later by a different emotion. I was fed up. Fed up of being scared, fed up of him misbehaving, fed up with the failures that I'd allowed to overshadow the successes we'd had.

"Just pack it in, would you?" I snapped, correcting Misty firmly with the reins before going into a steady rising trot, setting the pace with my own body and challenging him to meet me.

At first Misty argued, but as I circled and half-halted and changed the rein, as I slowed him down and allowed him forward then slowed him down again, as I rode transition after transition after transition, he eventually started to soften. The rest of the show, the rest of the world faded away, and I focused on Misty, and Misty alone. The shape of the circle that his hooves made in the damp grass, the arch of his neck in front of my hands, the curve of his body around my leg, the puffs of air that he blew out as he cantered, still just visible in the cool, still morning. It wasn't until I brought him back to a walk and let the reins go loose, reaching forward to pat his damp neck, that I looked over at Jonty. He was leaning up against a tree and watching me with a grin so wide that I thought his face might split in half.

I rode right up to him and halted Misty, who promptly used Jonty as a scratching post for his itchy head.

"Happy now?" I asked Jonty.

"Are you?"

I thought about that for a moment, then nodded. "Yeah. I'm still not ready to jump him, but I feel better. Like I just proved something…"

I broke off as my phone started ringing in my pocket. Misty jumped at the sound, and I gathered my reins in one hand and muttered at him as I extracted my phone. I expected it to be Katy or AJ, wondering where I'd gone, but it wasn't. It was Mum.

"Hello."

"Hi Tess. How's the show going?"

"Um…" I hadn't told her yet about Katy's accident. I wasn't sure why.

"Good," Mum filled in for me, proving that she barely listened to me anyway. "Well good news, Hayley's being discharged this morning."

"That's great!"

Mum kept talking as though I hadn't spoken. "And she's absolutely adamant that she's coming to see Misty jump. We're flying down at midday, and we're on track to arrive just before Pony of the Year starts. I don't know where he is in the draw but make sure he's well down to give us time, I'm sure people will accommodate given the circumstances."

"I…" I had to say something. I didn't know what to say. "Is that really a good idea?" I asked. "I mean, so soon…"

"Of course it's not a good idea, but it's what Hayley wants to do," Mum said, summing up my sister in one sentence. I heard someone talking in the background, and then she said "I have to go, I'll see you in a few hours. Make sure the truck's tidy and we can leave straightaway afterwards."

"Mum, listen…"

But she'd already hung up. I lowered my phone and slid it back into my pocket, then looked at Jonty, who was watching me with eyebrows lifted, curious.

"Hayley's coming to watch Misty jump this afternoon."

Jonty broke into a grin. "She's out of hospital?" I nodded, and he put a hand on my leg and squeezed it. "That's awesome."

"Yeah, it's great." I couldn't get my enthusiasm to resonate in my voice, and Jonty gave me a quizzical look. "I'm happy for her, I really am. But she's coming to see Misty jump."

He nodded, understanding. "I guess that means you have to make a decision," Jonty said, flicking his hair out of his eyes as he looked up at me. "Either you ring your mum back and tell her not to bother because you've scratched him, or you find someone else to ride him, or…" He hesitated, and I finished the sentence for him.

"Or I ride him myself."

His eyes flickered with excitement, but he just nodded slowly. "Or you ride him yourself."

I looked down at Misty's short fluffy mane, at the rubber-grip reins, at the thin layer of sweat on his neck. He tossed his head and snorted, then started pawing impatiently at the ground.

"I'll think about it."

"Well, you'd better hurry up," Jonty said, glancing at his watch. "The class starts in a few hours."

I rode Misty back to the yards, racking my brains frantically. The stabling area was a hive of activity, but our yards were all empty. AJ and Susannah must have taken the ponies out for a leg stretch and a pick of grass. I slid down from Misty's broad back and led him into the yard, then unbuckled his girth. Jonty removed Misty's bridle and slung it over the railing.

"What're you thinking?" he asked finally.

I shrugged. "I could ask Anna to ride him."

"You could." He couldn't hide his disappointment as he buckled Misty's halter onto his sweaty head. "Do you want to?"

"No."

Jonty turned to look at me, one eyebrow raised speculatively. "Well then."

"Well then." I hesitated for a moment longer, then looked at Misty. "What d'you reckon, Misty? Think we've got one more round left in us?"

Misty bunted me with his nose, knocking me backwards into the railing. I grabbed it with one hand, and Jonty grabbed my other arm to keep my balance.

"I think that was a most emphatic yes," I told Jonty, who laughed. "I think you're probably right."

My hands were shaking on the reins as I rode Misty towards the warm-up area. It was swarming with people and ponies, trotting and cantering around in the warm midday sun, kicking up clouds of dust while everyone who had already jumped stood around watching and reliving their rounds with varying degrees of excitement. Three practice fences stood side by side in the middle of the arena, one set as a crossrail, one as a vertical and the third as an oxer. I watched Anna canter Saxon down to the oxer and soar over it, and my pulse quickened.

"You good?" Jonty asked me as I halted Misty at the gate and anxiously checked my girth for the fifth time.

"No," I told him honestly. "But I'm trying to be."

He shot me a crooked grin, patting me reassuringly on the knee. Susannah trotted past, then circled Molly around and brought her back towards me with a smile.

"Hey, Tess. Come trot round with me."

I nudged Misty forward and he fell into step with Molly, who pulled a face at him. "How's she going?" I asked Susannah, trying to take my mind off what I was about to do.

"She's excited," Susannah said. "Not sure if that means she'll jump like a pro or slam on the brakes out there, but I guess I'll find out."

She shrugged, looking remarkably calm about the proposition of being thrown headfirst into a jump. Katy had handed her the ride last night after getting back from the hospital, and Susannah had willingly accepted. She'd ridden Molly before, and the bay mare had always gone well for her.

"I know how you feel," I said, shortening my reins another inch as Misty got up onto his toes. "I'm seriously regretting this decision."

"You'll be fine," Susannah insisted, echoing the same words that everyone had been telling me since I'd made my decision to compete public. "Just point him at the jumps and don't fall off."

I grinned at her. "Is that all?"

"All there is to it," she insisted as the steward came to the gate and started calling out the order.

"Sophie, down the chute, you're on next," he called, and a girl on an Appaloosa pony headed for the gate with a chorus of good luck calls following her. "Then it's Gemma, followed by Luke…" he continued, and I listened carefully for my name, which came at the end of the list. "Susannah six away, Jordan seven away, Tess eight away, and Anna will be the last to go."

Jonty came into the warm-up and stationed himself next to the crossrail, and I took a breath and touched Misty into a canter. It was time to forget about everything else, and just focus on the job I had to do. I hadn't jumped since my fall off Misty, with the exception of the gate that I'd had to kick Rory over, and I eyed the low cross nervously as Misty bounded towards it. I sank my weight down into my heels, kept my shoulders back, and looked over the fence as Misty popped over, landed smoothly and cantered on.

I let out a breath, and kept coming. Over it again, and again, and then on to the vertical, which Jonty had lowered to only about 80cm, and over that, and then over it at 90cm, and then at a metre. I brought Misty back to a trot and gave him a pat as Lily headed down the chute on her little palomino pony, and I tried to remember how many riders ahead of me she'd been.

"Tess!" Katy was standing by the rail and waving to me with her good arm, and I trotted Misty over to her. "Hayley and your mum are here. AJ's gone to meet them at the gate."

"Thanks."

I wasn't sure whether I was relieved that they'd arrived in time – albeit barely – or whether I was disappointed that they might see me fail. Katy smiled at me, then turned her head as Susannah rode

Molly down to the oxer. She saw a long spot and kicked on for it, but Molly hesitated, then slammed on the brakes, crashing into the poles and knocking them to the ground. Katy swore as Susannah gathered her reins up and Jonty went to rebuild the fence. Misty jibbed impatiently, so I let him trot on again, circling at one end of the arena while the fence was put back up. Susannah was called down the chute just then, but her father started yelling at the steward to wait as he hurried over to help Jonty reset the fence. Katy coached Susannah over the vertical, which Molly cleared effortlessly, then circled back around to the oxer. This time she met it on a good stride, but once again, Molly refused.

"This is going to be a disaster," I heard Katy say as I cantered by.

Susannah tried again, managing to get Molly to jump this time, but taking the back rail with her as she went. The steward insisted that she was out of time to try again, and she headed down the chute with a rueful expression.

"Your turn," Jonty told me. "Don't overthink it. Just go."

He'd lowered the rails substantially so the jump was only about a metre-ten, but it looked immense. *You've jumped that height loads of times*, I told myself. *And way bigger. Shut up and do it.*

And I did. I focused on the same three things as before – heels down, shoulders back, eyes up – and before I knew it, Misty and I were safely on the other side. I patted the pony gratefully, then circled around and jumped it again. My heart was still racing but I was starting to feel more confident, even as Jonty lifted the rails until they were level with his shoulder.

Heels down, shoulders back, eyes up.

One, two, three, jump.

Easy, right?

Moments later I was heading down the chute as Susannah was riding back up, with Katy walking alongside her.

"How'd you go?" I asked, though I could tell from the looks on their faces that the answer was somewhere in the realm of 'not great'.

"She didn't fall off," Katy told me. "So – better than me. Good luck."

"Thanks." I walked Misty down and halted him at the gate, taking a deep breath. Jonty was right next to me, his hand on my knee, looking out across the course. I had no idea where Hayley and Mum were, had no idea whether they'd even made it ringside in time to watch.

"What if they miss it?" I asked Jonty, my voice panicking.

"They'll see you go again in the second round," he said assuredly, but I couldn't return his confidence, figuring that the chances of me making into the second round were slim to none.

I felt physically sick, and turned my head away from him, wondering whether I could vomit off the side of Misty without the pony freaking out. I felt bile rising in my throat, and swallowed hard.

"In you go," the steward told me with an encouraging smile. "Good luck. You deserve it."

Jonty's hand patted me on the knee, then Misty moved forward, passing under the dark green Farmlands archway into the arena. He wasn't nervous at all – he was thrilled to be there, the centre of everyone's attention. As the previous rider cantered down to the last fence on course, I took a moment to look around at the grandstand, packed to capacity, at the multiple flags and banners that surrounded the ring, at the people leaning on the railings, watching with interest, wondering who would go on to win the most prestigious pony class in the country. And down below my terror, below the nausea and the cold sweat trickling down my back, part of me was standing up and cheering too.

The hooter sounded, and Misty half-reared, sinking his weight back onto his hocks. I dissociated myself from my fear and focused forward, thinking only of where the first fence was and my need to get to it. I was vaguely aware of the loudspeaker announcing my name as Misty leapt forward into a pounding canter.

"Tessa Maxwell…Misty Magic."

For a fleeting moment I wished I could see the look on Hayley's face right now, and then I forced myself to concentrate. The first fence was a green and white oxer on the far side of the arena, and I rode Misty towards it with only three things on my mind.

Heels down, shoulders back, eyes up.

We cleared the first, and cantered on to the second. It was a rustic vertical and it looked suddenly huge as we approached it. I felt my body tense up, felt myself hesitate, but Misty didn't. He powered forward and leapt over, racing forward in his eager search for the next jump.

"Woah," I murmured to him, tightening my grip on the reins.

Fence three was a huge oxer down in front of the grandstand. It looked immense, impossible, unjumpable. I gritted my teeth and put my leg on, but two strides out from the jump we both knew that we were on a bad distance. A fleeting instinct told me to pull Misty away from the jump and circle him, but I knew that if I allowed my fear to overwhelm me, I would never be able to talk myself into a second attempt. So I took the only other option I felt that I had – to clamp my legs against Misty's side, grab his mane, close my eyes and let the chips fall where they may.

I felt his muscles bunch beneath me, felt his hindquarters sink down and then his shoulders coming up to meet me. I leaned forward, following the movement of the pony as he propelled himself off the ground and stretched out over the jump. In mid-air, I opened my eyes again, but instantly regretted it. Misty had left the ground early, but there was no way he was going to clear the back rail from that distance. Sure enough, his front hooves knocked the pole from its cups as he began his descent, landing on the ground in front of us and ready to trip Misty up. I sucked in a breath but Misty just put in some fancy footwork, skipping over the pole and cantering on, his ears laid back in irritation. He hated taking rails.

I reached one hand forward and gave him a thankful pat for saving my skin, then turned towards the one-stride double. We'd made it over, and now I was embarrassed by what I'd just done, leaving it all up to him and taking no responsibility. We were supposed to be a team, and I was acting like a passenger. *Get it together, Tess!*

I sat down in the saddle and tried to let my body meld into Misty's. I saw the strides coming into the double, and we jumped cleanly through the combination, then powered down to the triple bar and soared over that as well. Pleased with himself, Misty bucked all the way around the corner, but I was ready for him, and dug my knees in tight. I pulled his head up and straightened him just in time for the wall, then sat back and held him for the bending line to the planks. For the first time ever, Misty responded immediately when I asked him to slow down, and although he tapped the top plank with one hoof, it stayed up.

I was doing better, but every time I saw a jump in front of me I still felt my heart seize, still couldn't breathe properly until we'd landed, and then only until the next fence was lined up, when it started all over again. I couldn't wait to be finished, couldn't wait to get out of the ring and have it over and done with. We cantered around the turn, and I fixed my eyes on the skinny white gate that lay ahead. I could hear someone yelling from the sidelines, and abruptly realised that I was heading for the wrong jump. There was a red oxer to my right that I had to jump next, and without pausing to think, without considering my safety or measuring up the angle or worrying at all about whether or not it was possible, I swung Misty towards it and clicked my tongue, my heels digging into his round sides.

Misty never hesitated. He simply took three strides, sat back on his hocks and leapt. We cleared the wide oxer on a sharp angle that I would never have attempted even in a jump off, and I could hear the crowd gasping and then clapping as we landed safely on the other side. Adrenalin surged through me, and I rode Misty on towards the white gate. I hadn't come all this way to do something as stupid as forget the course, and I met the next fence with a new determination. Misty rose to meet me, and we finally clicked. We took the rest of the course as one, bounding through the treble, jumping the final oxer with room to spare, and charging through the finish flags. Misty fired off a series of characteristic celebratory bucks, and as I heard the crowd cheering, I couldn't believe that I'd done it. Adrenalin had taken over and pushed me way outside my comfort zone, somehow breaking through the fear barrier that had been holding me back. I steadied Misty into his high-stepping trot and headed for the gate, passing the red oxer as we went. I looked over at it incredulously. When I'd walked the course, I'd avoided looking at how wide it was, at how high it was. I could've ridden Misty between the front and back rails without touching either of them, but we'd flown over it effortlessly. Overcome with gratitude for Misty's courage, I leaned forward and hugged his arched neck, aware at last of just how incredibly lucky I was to be riding this pony.

Hayley had been right all along about him, and I looked around for her as I reached the exit gate, where Jonty was waiting for me with an ear-splitting grin. Susannah and Katy were right beside him, their voices ringing out with congratulations as they grabbed Misty's reins and dragged me out of the saddle for congratulatory hugs.

"I told you he went better for you," Susannah said.

"That was so good!" Katy exclaimed, hugging me with one arm before Jonty grabbed me and hugged me tight. I squeezed him back as hard as I could for a long moment before we stepped back and looked at each other with matching grins.

"Phew," I said, and he laughed.

"Man, I almost had a heart attack when you missed at fence three," he told me.

"I had my eyes closed the whole time," I admitted, making him laugh again.

"Never mind fence three, what about the red oxer?" Katy demanded. "We thought you were going straight past it, and then you just took it at the most insane angle I've ever seen!"

I unclipped my helmet and pulled it off my sweaty head.

"I forgot the course," I told her. "Almost missed it, but Misty is a superstar and made it work somehow."

"I couldn't believe he still jumped it," Katy said, and I shook my head as Susannah led Misty away to cool him off. His thick white tail swished from side to side as he strolled along next to her, and I smiled as he pushed her sideways with his head, knocking her off balance.

"Neither can I."

I heard my name called and turned to see AJ running up to me.

"Tess!" She flung herself over the barrier and hugged me tight. "You were amazing! Come on, they're down here," she said, grabbing my hand and dragging me behind her.

I followed, my legs feeling shaky again as I wondered what the verdict was from my family. I'd screwed up fence three, I knew that, and my sense of shame was returning. The rail had been my fault – if I'd got it together sooner, if I'd concentrated harder, if I'd balanced him better out of the turn, he wouldn't have missed. If I hadn't just sat there with my eyes closed...

AJ pulled me sideways and then stopped, and I came face to face with my sister. She was paler than usual, with dark circles under her eyes and a tension in her shoulders that betrayed how much pain she was in. She was sitting in a plastic chair beside the ring, her hands clasped together and elbows on the table while a large umbrella sheltered her from the sun. A bright pink cap sat on top of the long blonde curls that tumbled down her back, and her expression was unreadable behind large sunglasses.

"You." She lifted a hand from the table and pointed a shaky finger at me. A couple of people's heads turned as Hayley slowly shook her head, then broke into a huge grin. "That was the best thing I've ever seen."

Tears sprang to my eyes, and a lump rose in my throat. "Really?"

Hayley stood up and opened her arms, and I stepped into them for a hug. Her embrace was weak and she held me gently, her cheek pressed against mine.

"I've never been so proud of you. You did great."

I felt the tears escape from under my eyelids as I hugged her back. I hadn't felt this close to her for years, and a sudden memory seized me, from when I'd fallen off my bike and scraped my knee when I was little. I'd burst into tears, but Hayley had wiped away my tears and told me not to cry, because she would look after me. We broke apart and smiled at each other as I wiped my eyes.

"I had a rail," I reminded her as she sat back down and Mum grabbed me for a quick congratulatory hug.

"I know. Bugger. Saw it coming," Hayley said. "But AJ says there's only been one clear round so far, so you're definitely through to round two."

"Really?" I asked AJ, who nodded.

"Yeah," she said, her eyes flickering towards Hayley as she spoke. "Susannah was clear on Skip!"

I broke into a smile. "That's great! Good for her."

Hayley was distracted by Mum, who was fussing over her, something Hayley never tolerated much. "I'm fine, Mum. Leave me alone for five seconds, would you? If you have to do something, go get me and Tess one of those berry smoothies each. AJ too," she added, glancing at my friend.

"I'm fine, I'm going to go find Katy," AJ said.

"And I should get back to Misty," I added, but AJ shook her head.

"Jonty's got him, he's fine," she assured me. "I'll come find you if we need you."

So she left, Mum went to buy us smoothies, and Hayley told me to sit down. I took Mum's vacated seat and looked at my sister.

"You look good."

"Don't lie, Tess," she said. "I look like crap. But I don't care. Not anymore." She sighed and looked around. "Man, I've missed this. This is what it's all about, isn't it?"

I nodded. "It's pretty good."

"Pretty good?" she asked incredulously. "It's everything. It's life. And I'll be back out there before you know it. Just you watch."

"I know you will," I agreed as the course designers started resetting the course for round two.

"Soon," Hayley promised, talking more to herself now than to me. "Very soon."

15

FEARLESS

I left Hayley to go and walk the course for the second round. Susannah was walking the course with her trainer Bruce, so Katy came with me. We paced out the combinations, discussed the lines that were set and where to shave the corners to save precious seconds, as the time allowed would be much tighter in this round.

"I'll probably fall off before I even get this far," I told Katy as we paced out the treble.

She responded by reaching out and smacking the back of my head. "Enough of that defeatist attitude," she said. "I'm not walking the course with a broken wrist just to amuse myself, you know."

"Sorry." I looked at the third fence in the combination, an immense oxer that followed the two verticals leading in, and tried for a better attitude. "I'm going to jump a clear round this time."

"Damn straight. Just kick on, keep your eyes open, and let your pony do his job."

Twenty riders were called back, and I was second to last to go, so I went back to sit with Hayley to see how the course rode. She passed me a smoothie, and I took a sip as the hooter sounded.

"And we're ready to get underway now with our first rider in the second round, Lily Christianson riding Westbrook Double Happy."

"She had two stops on the palomino," Hayley said as Lily cantered her opening circle. "And eight faults on this one. Probably the first eight fault round that pony's had in its life."

"She made it into the team to go to Ireland," I commented as Lily knocked down the first fence.

"I know. How stupid is that? I told Mum you should've put your name forward."

"They'd never have taken me," I said.

"True, I suppose. Anyway, it's all political, that stuff. You need to have enough pull with the selectors. How else do you explain Lily getting in?"

I shrugged. "She had good results at Nationals."

"Oh please, that was a fluke," Hayley said dismissively. "The team's a joke. Katy's all right, but if they really wanted the juniors to win, they would've picked Susannah." I shot her a surprised look, and she shrugged. "I don't have to like her to admit that she can ride. She's come a long way in the last few years, and she's a helluva lot better than *that*," Hayley opined, pointing at Lily as she chipped into the wall and knocked the top block off it. "She's racking up a cricket score out there on the most pushbutton pony on the circuit."

"She's definitely not having the best round," I agreed diplomatically.

We watched in silence as Lily finished, giving Happ a rueful pat as she trotted to the gate and Grace Campbell came in on her experienced dark bay. She started well, but Summertime fumbled at the treble and had all three fences down. She was followed by Stacey Winchester, who took out the first and last fences on her pretty black gelding, then a girl called Sophie on a spotted Appaloosa jumped clear within the time. The crowd rewarded her with raucous applause, and Sophie patted her pony exuberantly.

"Settle down, jeez," Hayley muttered. "She's still sitting on eight from the first round, let's not get too excited."

But the rails kept coming down, and when I left to get back on Misty, Sophie's was still only the only clear in the second round.

I trotted and cantered Misty around the warm-up, trying to stay calm. Susannah would be last to go, as the only clear in the first round, and if she could repeat the feat, she would get the win without taking it to a jump off.

"Anna, down the chute. Tess, you're after her, then Susannah's last to go."

Susannah nodded as she cantered past on her glossy chestnut pony, looking as polished and professional as ever. Anna trotted Saxon through the gate, and I rode Misty over to where Jonty was standing.

"How're you feeling?" he asked.

"I just want it to be over," I admitted to him as I leaned forward and patted Misty's neck. "One more round, mate," I told the pony. "Just one more, then we're done for the season." *Probably forever*, I thought, but I didn't want to say that out loud.

"Don't tell him that, you'll break his heart," Jonty teased me. "Besides, if you go clear and Susannah pulls a rail, you could have to jump off against her."

"If that happens, I'd concede defeat," I told him. "I'm not sure how many more times I can do this."

Before Jonty could speak, the steward called over to me.

"Tess, you ready?" I nodded, and he gestured toward the gate. "Down the chute, then. Good luck."

I walked down to the archway with Jonty by my side, leaving Susannah to finish her warm-up. I could see the excitement on people's faces as I passed them, as they wished me luck and whispered to each other. It'd make a great story – the girl whose sister had a brain tumour winning Pony of the Year – but I didn't want to be a headline. I knew that winning mattered to Hayley, mattered to Mum, probably even mattered to Jonty more than it did to me. It definitely mattered more to Susannah, who'd been chasing this title since she was eleven, and to Anna, who was taking her last shot at it before moving off ponies. But it didn't matter to me. I just wanted to make it over all of the jumps.

I halted Misty under the arch, and he pawed the ground impatiently. The crowd was quiet, and as Anna tapped the triple bar, a soft gasp issued from the grandstand. But the fence stayed up, and she jumped Saxon cleanly down the treble, then cantered on to the final oxer. The crowd held its collective breath as they landed cleanly and raced through the flags, then erupted into applause.

"That's a clear round within the time for Anna Harcourt and Six of One!" the commentator said excitedly as I trotted Misty into the ring. "Next to go will be Misty Magic, ridden by Tessa Maxwell, and if they can jump clear as well, we will have a jump off!"

The crowd murmured excitedly. Everyone loved a jump off. The buzzer sounded, and I touched Misty into a canter, eyeing the first fence.

Forget everything else.

Ignore the crowd, block out the noise.

Heels down.

Shoulders back.

Eyes up…

Misty flew over the first fence, and over the second. I steered him around the course, doing my best to stay with him, but letting him make the decisions about where to take off from. I put my fate into his hands, so to speak, and he took care of me. He truly was a phenomenal pony, and I liked him more with every fence we cleared. He no longer hauled at the reins around the corners, no longer spooked and shimmied and shot forward with the least provocation. We were finally working as a team, and as we came around the corner to the treble, I realised that we only had four fences left to clear. If we made it over all of them, we would be in a jump off against Anna. For a fleeting second, I was excited by the prospect. Then a kid leaning over the railing dropped their shopping bag into the ring. It landed with a rustle, and Misty spooked, jumping sideways with his eyes bugging out. I pulled his head around to straighten him, clicking my tongue furiously to attempt to get his attention back, but he had lost focus.

"Misty, come on!"

I tapped him on the shoulder with the short crop that I carried, and he shot forward. We were coming into the treble fast and flat now, and I dug my knees into the saddle and held on, forcing myself to keep my eyes open, praying that we would make it safely through.

Misty jumped awkwardly over the first, and I lost a stirrup on landing. There was no time to get it back, so I just grabbed his mane and held on, but he'd lost his momentum and hit the brakes, sliding across the grass and knocking the jump down with his barrel chest. The crowd groaned, the hooter sounded, and I managed to regain my stirrup as Misty backed out of the scattered poles. Ring stewards came running over to rebuild the jump, and I ran my hand down Misty's neck as he jogged nervously away.

"You're okay," I told him, talking as much to myself as I was to the pony. "It was just a little mistake. We're fine. We're okay."

It was the worst case scenario for me. A rail I could've handled, but a refusal was a completely different confidence crisis. I gritted my teeth, determined not to let it rattle me. We could still do this, could still make it home. We weren't going to give up.

The seconds seemed to stretch into hours as the jump was slowly rebuilt, the course builder gave the starter the thumbs up, and the hooter sounded again. I pressed Misty back into a canter, my hands clenched around the reins, pulse racing. It was all down to Misty now, and whether he decided to jump or not. I knew that I didn't have the determination to force him down the line. I wasn't like Hayley, who would've got the whip out and given him a good smack behind her leg before restarting, who would've ridden down that treble with her reins in one hand if she'd needed to, throwing every fibre of her being over the fence in front of her, consumed with determination. I had to trust that Misty would do it for me because he wanted to be good, because I asked him nicely, because he trusted me too. Six months ago, he wouldn't even have considered it. Six weeks ago he probably wouldn't have either, but a lot had changed since then. I wasn't scared of him anymore. It was the jumping, not the pony, that frightened me, I realised as I cantered towards the treble. And that made all the difference in the world.

We were slightly deep to the first, and I heard Hayley yelling as we landed.

"KICK!"

I squeezed Misty with my legs and clicked my tongue, and he bounded forward and flew over the second jump, then took two strides and cleared the third. Six forward strides down to the final oxer, and we met it well, and then we were in the air, and I felt a whoosh of air rush out of my lungs as I realised that we'd done it.

My friends met me at the gate, smiling and saying "well done" and "nice recovery" and "at least you got over it the second time". I just smiled, overwhelmed with relief that it was done and dusted, then wished Susannah luck as she cantered into the ring. She was the last rider to go, only needing a clear round to win. Her father stood at the gate, knuckles in his mouth, watching her.

I dismounted and ran up Misty's stirrups, then hugged him around his sweaty neck.

"Best pony," I told him. "Best in the world."

Jonty was grinning at me as he took Misty's reins over his head. "I'll walk him out for you," he offered. "You stay and watch Susannah."

"Sure?"

"Yeah. Go on."

He nudged me back towards my friends and I went to stand with them. AJ put her arm around my waist and squeezed me in towards her.

"You did good."

"Thanks."

"Glad you decided to do it?" Katy asked me, her eyes still fixed on Susannah as she cantered down to the first fence.

"Now that it's over, yeah," I admitted, and Katy laughed.

"It'll get easier," she assured me, then sucked in a sharp breath as Skip rattled the top rail of the first fence.

It stayed up though, and Susannah continued down to the second. We watched anxiously, hearts in our mouths as Skip jumped the entire course seemingly by braille, tapping every rail, but miraculously, none of them fell. It wasn't until she was out of the treble and on her way to the last, and everyone was holding their breath because she was only one fence away from winning the long-desired Pony of the Year title without even having to do a jump off, that her luck ran out. Skip missed his distance, went long, and rubbed the front rail of the oxer. It rolled out of the cups and hit the ground, and the crowd sighed with disappointment, then immediately started chattering with excitement as the commentator reminded them of what that meant.

"Ladies and gentlemen, there will be a jump off!"

We went straight to Susannah's side, offering vague platitudes as she patted her pony ruefully on her way out of the gate. Her father marched behind us, looking bitterly disappointed.

"You can still win it," I reminded Susannah as she dismounted and leaned her face against Skip's sweaty neck. "It's not over yet, and Saxon's had an off week until now. He could easily fall apart."

"Just go faster than her and leave all the fences up," AJ said. "Easy."

Susannah laughed, straightening up and giving her pony a hug. "Well, when you say it like *that*," she replied, rolling her eyes. "God, I'm so nervous. I wish I could just fast-forward to the end and find out what happens."

"You smoke her and take out the win," Katy said confidently, and AJ spoke at the same time, offering a different outcome.

"She jumps clear and you fall off."

"I like Katy's version better," Susannah said before turning towards her father, who was coming over with Bruce, ready to discuss jump off tactics.

I left them to it. Jonty was leading Misty around the outside of the warm-up, and I went to meet them. Misty whinnied softly to me as I approached him, and I smiled.

"You are kinda cute, in your own obnoxious way," I told the pony as I reached his side.

"Thanks," Jonty said, and I grinned at him. He wrapped his arms around me and pulled me in for a hug. "You did awesome. You know that, right?"

"I do."

"Be proud of yourself."

"I am."

"Good."

We walked together for a few minutes before the announcer declared that the jump off was ready to start, and Anna would be the first to go. Jonty nudged me towards the ring.

"You should go watch. See Susannah win."

I ran back down the chute as Anna trotted into the arena. Susannah was sitting on Skip, talking to Bruce on one side as her father stood on the other, his hand resting on Skip's hogged mane. I couldn't see AJ and Katy, so I went back to where Hayley and Mum were sitting.

"There you are!" Mum exclaimed as I reached her. "We've been wondering where you got to. Where's Misty?"

"With Jonty." I moved closer to my sister, leaning on the railing next to her and watching Anna start her round.

Hayley spoke to me, though her eyes were fixed on her friend. "He really likes you, you know."

I frowned. "Jonty?"

"No, you egg. Misty. I thought for sure you were a goner when you had that stop," she said honestly. "I was surprised you stayed on, but I thought for sure he'd quit again the second time. But he went, because he likes you."

"Because he's the best," I said.

Hayley broke into a grin, put an arm around my shoulders and squeezed. "You've finally seen the light!"

"I guess so." I leaned into her embrace. "It's weird, but after he went home with Katy, I missed him. And I think he missed us too. I guess it's true that you don't know what you've got 'til it's gone."

"Ain't that the truth," Hayley muttered. "Come on Anna, put your foot down!"

We watched, shoulder to shoulder, as Anna raced Saxon around the course, slicing a couple of tight turns and leaving all of the fences up in a very smart time. The crowd cheered, Anna punched the air in triumph, and Susannah cantered into the ring with a determined expression. This was it, and she had to go clear – and faster than Anna – to win.

My heart was racing as I watched, holding my breath over every fence. Skip was jumping cleaner this time without tapping the rails and she was taking tight inside turns, but Anna had done that too, and I glanced at the clock as Skip landed off the wall, with only the oxer left to jump. It was going to be close, and I gasped as Susannah pushed her pony forward, making up time the only way she could, by taking the final fence at a gallop. I could hear the crowd's collective intake of breath, felt Hayley's arm tighten across my back, and watched as Skip took off. He was tidy in front, and the crowd started to cheer, but he tapped the back rail with one hind hoof. The pole wobbled once, twice, then settled back into the cups as Susannah raced Skip through the finish flags, and I looked up at the clock to see that she'd beaten Anna's time by half a second.

She had won.

I lay in bed that night with the curtains open, staring up at the stars.

We'd headed home straight after the class ended, loading Misty onto our truck and driving back to Waipukurau. The celebrations would be going on well into the night in Susannah's truck, and I wondered what my friends were doing now, and whether they were missing me.

A cool breeze wafted through the open window as I replayed the events of the day in my mind. The early morning ride on the polo field, the decision to ride Misty myself, the nerves and nausea that had followed. The paralysing fear as I went into the ring, and the overwhelming relief as I rode out. The incredible sensation of flying when Misty and I found the right spot to a fence, the way the crowd had cheered on our victory lap, because despite Misty's refusal, we'd still finished in fourth place. The wide green sash was already pinned on my wall, and I stared at it in amazement, bewildered that I could have done such a thing.

My phone buzzed, and I fumbled for it, squinting at the bright screen as my eyes adjusted.

Katy O'Reilly tagged you in a photo.

I tapped the screen and waited for the picture to load. The professional photographers had been quick to upload pictures from the class, and I'd already looked at dozens of pictures of Misty soaring over ridiculously large jumps with me looking inexplicably poised in the saddle. So far, nobody had caught me with my eyes shut, which I was eternally grateful for. But this one wasn't a jumping photo. It had been snapped as Susannah and I were riding side-by-side out of the arena after the presentation. Susannah was grinning from ear to ear, the winner's garland hanging around Skip's shoulders, and AJ was walking between us with one arm over Skip's neck and a huge smile on her face. Katy was on Susannah's other side, her arm in its sling, looking up at Susannah proudly. Jonty was next to me, one hand reaching into his pocket for a peppermint, and Misty had his head turned towards him, eyes bright with anticipation of the treat. I zoomed in on the picture, scrolling slowly back and forth across our smiling faces as a warm feeling built inside me. The five of us had been friends for a while now, but after the past few days at HOY, we'd become more than that. We'd become a team, and the photo proved it.

And that wasn't the only good picture to come from the show. There was a great shot of Misty jumping the triple bar that Mum fell in love with. She had it framed and hung it in the entrance hall for everyone to comment on as soon as they entered the house, and most people did. It was a great photo, catching Misty at the height of his jump, his knees tucked in tight and ears pricked forward. Yet no matter how many times I looked at it, I still couldn't quite believe that it was me. The girl in that photo looked competent. Focused. Fearless, as though she was born to do this.

She looked like Hayley.

For my bedroom wall, I chose a different picture, one that told a different story. The story of a girl who was everything but fearless. A girl who could never have done any of it on her own – and who only succeeded, in the end, once she realised that she didn't have to.

♥

GLOSSARY OF TERMS

Bottle lambs – lambs that were orphaned or rejected by their mothers at birth, who were raised on bottled milk formula, e.g. Mildred and Myrtle.

Come away – working dog command meaning 'go right'.

Come by – working dog command meaning 'go left'.

Drenching – necessary to treat and prevent worms and other parasites; can be an oral drench squirted into the animal's mouth, a pour-on drench which is squirted along their back, or a dip, where the sheep runs under a spray of diluted drench.

Farm hack – a horse bred and/or trained for farm work. Also known as a station hack, or stationbred. Mixed bloodlines, often contains some Clydesdale for bone and Standardbred for smooth paces.

Gallipoli – site of battle during WWI in 1915 where 2,779 New Zealanders were killed, and 5,212 injured. The Australian and New Zealand troops were known collectively as ANZACs, and their sacrifice, and that of our soldiers in any other wards, are commemorated every year on April 25th, known as ANZAC Day. Tess's family named several sites on the farm after Gallipoli.

Heading dog / eye dog – Bred from the border collie, heading dogs are discouraged from barking, instead using their speed and agility to keep the stock together, often by eyeballing them at close quarters to hold them in place (hence the name 'eye dog'). Excellent in close quarter situations, and have very quick reaction times. Usually black and white.

Heifer – an adult cow who has not yet calved.

Hoggets – a lamb between weaning and first shearing, between 1 to 2 years of age.

Huntaway – Big, strong dogs that are bred for their loud bark which encourages stock to move away from them. Used for all aspects of farm work. Usually black and tan. Cave and Thor, who accompany the girls on their muster, are Huntaways.

Keep out – working dog command meaning 'cast your circle wider to gather more sheep'.

Race/Raceway – a narrow section in stock yards where stock can be shut in at close quarters, making it easier to drench, vaccinated etc. Also a fenced track between paddocks, wide enough for a tractor to get through.

Smoko – a colloquial term for a break for food (and/or cigarette, hence the name); can be used for morning tea, afternoon tea, or any other time you feel like stopping.

Station/Sheep station – a big farm.

Switchback – a trail that cuts back and forth across a hill in a zig-zag formation.

Two-tooths – sheep who have two teeth, usually around 2 years of age.

Weaner calves – beef calves, aged between seven and eight months, who are weaned off their mothers and sold to other farmers to be fattened for the beef market.

Woolshed – a big shed used for shearing. Necessary on sheep farms, especially big ones. Some include kitchen facilities and a place to sleep, though some farms also have separate shearer's quarters. Sheep are shorn twice annually, once in spring and again before tupping (when the ram goes out) in late summer.

Pony Jumpers - Special Edition #1
JONTY

Jonty Fisher hasn't grown up with horses. Hasn't grown up with much of anything, tell you the truth, except a love for being outdoors and a restless energy he can't quite contain. The unexpected arrival of a bedraggled black pony on his eleventh birthday marks the beginning of a new direction in his life, setting him on a path that will determine what he can make of his future.

But as Jonty's desire to prove himself builds, the school of hard knocks never fails to keep pushing him back down, and it will take a lot of courage, resilience and heart for him to find a way to follow his dreams.

Still, if life was meant to be easy, everyone would do it…

ABOUT THE AUTHOR

Kate Lattey lives in Waikanae, New Zealand and started riding at the age of 10. She was lucky enough to have ponies of her own during her teenage years, and competed regularly in show jumping, eventing and mounted games before finishing college and heading to university, graduating with a Bachelor of Arts in English & Media Studies.

In the years since, she has never been far from horses, and has worked in various jobs including as a livery yard groom in England, a trekking guide in Ireland, a riding school manager in New Zealand, and a summer camp counselor in the USA. It was during her time there that Kate started writing short stories about the camp's horses, which were a huge hit with the campers, and inspired Kate to continue pursuing her passion for writing.

Kate currently owns a Welsh Cob x Thoroughbred gelding named JJ, and competes in show jumping and show hunter competitions, as well as coaching at Pony Club and judging at local events.

She has been reading and writing pony stories ever since she can remember, and has many more yet to come! If you enjoyed this book, check out the rest of the series and her other novels on Amazon, and visit nzponywriter.com to sign up for her mailing list and get information about new and upcoming releases.

DARE TO DREAM

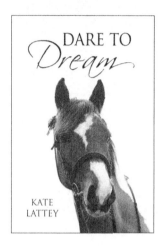

Saying goodbye to the horses they love has become a way of life for Marley and her sisters, who train and sell show jumpers to make their living. Marley has grand ambitions to jump in Pony of the Year, but every good pony she's ever had has been sold out from under her to pay the bills.

Then a half-wild pinto pony comes into her life, and Marley finds that this most unlikely of champions could be the superstar she has always dreamed of. As Marley and Cruise rise quickly to the top of their sport, it seems as though her dream might come true after all.

But her family is struggling to make ends meet, and as the countdown to Pony of the Year begins, Marley is forced to face the possibility of losing the pony she has come to love more than anything else in the world.

Can Marley save the farm she loves, without sacrificing the pony she can't live without?

DREAM ON

"Nobody has ever tried to understand this pony.
Nobody has ever been on her side. Until now.
She needs you to fight for her, Marley. She needs you to love her."

Borderline Majestic was imported from the other side of the world to bring her new owners fame and glory, but she is almost impossible to handle and ride. When the pony lands her rider in intensive care, it is up to Marley to prove that the talented mare is not dangerous - just deeply misunderstood.

Can Marley dare to fall in love again to save Majestic's life?

This much-anticipated sequel to *Dare to Dream* was a Top 20 Kindle Book Awards Semi-Finalist in 2015.

Clearwater Bay #1
FLYING CHANGES

When Jay moves from her home in England to live with her estranged father in rural New Zealand, it is only his promise of a pony of her own that convinces her to leave her old life behind and start over in a new country.

Change doesn't come easily at first, and Jay makes as many enemies as she does friends before she finds the perfect pony, who seems destined to make her dreams of show jumping success come true.

But she soon discovers that training her own pony is not as easy as she thought it would be, and her dream pony is becoming increasingly unmanageable and difficult to ride.

Can Jay pull it all together, or has she made the biggest mistake of her life?

Clearwater Bay #2
AGAINST THE CLOCK

It's a new season and a new start for Jay and her wilful pony Finn, but their best laid plans are quickly plagued by injuries, arguments and rails that just won't stay in their cups. And when her father introduces her to his new girlfriend, Jay can't help wondering if her life will ever run according to plan.

While her friends battle with their own families and Jay struggles to define hers, it is only her determination to bring out the best in her pony that keeps her going. But after overhearing a top rider say that Finn's potential is being hampered by her incompetent rider, Jay is besieged by doubts in her own ability…and begins to wonder whether Finn would be better off without her.

Can Jay bear to give up on her dreams, even if it's for her pony's sake?

Also by Kate Lattey

PONY JUMPERS

DARE TO DREAM

CLEARWATER BAY

For more information, visit nzponywriter.com

Email nzponywriter@gmail.com and sign up to my mailing list for exclusive previews, new releases, giveaways and more!

Printed in Great Britain
by Amazon